"Why don't you believe me?"

His eyes moved over April's face as if he were touching her. "Because you are too desirable to be real," Michalis said bitterly. "Too young, too beautiful to be what you seem. You came to Greece with a ticket and little else. You were escaping a life you did not want and were expecting to stay permanently."

"If that's what you believe, then believe it. What does it matter, after all?"

"Perhaps it matters to me," Michalis muttered fiercely.

Patricia Wilson was born in Yorkshire and lived there until she married and had four children. She loves traveling and has lived in Singapore, Africa and Spain. She had always wanted to be a writer, but a growing family and career as a teacher left her with little time to pursue her interest. With the encouragement of her family she gave up teaching in order to concentrate on writing and her other interests of music and painting.

Don't miss any of our special offers. Write to us at the following address for information on our newest releases.

Harlequin Reader Service
U.S.: 3010 Walden Ave., P.O. Box 1325, Buffalo, NY 14269
Canadian: P.O. Box 609, Fort Erie, Ont. L2A 5X3

PASSIONATE CAPTIVITY
Patricia Wilson

Harlequin Books

TORONTO • NEW YORK • LONDON
AMSTERDAM • PARIS • SYDNEY • HAMBURG
STOCKHOLM • ATHENS • TOKYO • MILAN
MADRID • WARSAW • BUDAPEST • AUCKLAND

ISBN 0-373-03346-X

PASSIONATE CAPTIVITY

Copyright © 1993 by Patricia Wilson.

CHAPTER ONE

'I THINK I've almost finished. Pass up that last curtain, will you, Dora?' April Stewart perched precariously on top of the high steps and leaned forward as her friend hurried to obey.

'Be careful, for heaven's sake!' Dora yelped. 'I can't spare the time to take you to hospital.'

'Stop fussing. I know these steps as I know myself; they're mine. Anyway, I'm used to climbing. Heights don't bother me.'

April took the heavy curtain and proceeded to drape it expertly. She had only clearing up to do and the whole house was decorated and very subtly altered. It was all she could afford but it looked good. The windows were spectacular and the settees and chairs looked brand new in their fine covers.

The fact that it almost left her penniless wasn't bothering her too much at the moment—providing she didn't think too deeply about it. As a wedding present this refurbishing was perhaps a bit over-the-top, but her mother deserved it and she would at least have a lovely place to come back to and face any battle.

'It's beautiful,' Dora mused as April came safely to the floor and looked around with satisfaction. 'I wish I could afford you.'

'I wish anyone could. Times are hard at the moment and people have too many things to do with their money. Employing an interior designer is the last thing on their list. I haven't had an enquiry for weeks. There's the one next month and that's it.'

'You've paid for this yourself, haven't you?' Dora asked as they moved to the kitchen for coffee. 'You've done this whole house and used your own money.'

'It's for Mum,' April pointed out. 'It's a wedding present. She deserves it.'

'Well, she's going to get a big surprise. As wedding presents go, it's handsome. Now all you have to do is starve for a while and everything will be just fine.'

April had to agree that the idea had entered her mind. Doing the house had more or less emptied her account but she had felt the need to take some positive action. Life was going to be quite difficult for her mother for a long time, as far as she could see. Not that her mother had made a wrong choice in Edwin Burton. He was charming, kind and amusing, and her mother was so obviously in love with him that things should have been blissful.

It was Edwin's seventeen-year-old daughter who would stir up the trouble, and April had no doubts about that. Gail Burton moved about like a black cloud, resenting everything and everybody. The resentment definitely extended to Edwin's new wife and fastened quite ferociously on April.

'You'll have a new sister here a week from now,' Dora pointed out with a sideways glance at April. 'All jolly sulks and frowns.'

'Mum will be facing that, not me,' April reminded her. 'I have my own flat.'

'But you'll have to be round here from time to time. Your mother's used to you popping in and out. If you simply stay away she's going to think you don't like Edwin.'

'She knows differently. Things can't be normal for a while. If I come as often as usual, Gail will be more awkward than she is now. They want time to themselves until Gail accepts Mum. After that she might just accept me.' April tried to look serene and hopeful. 'In any case, I'm getting out of the way for a couple of weeks. I think Gail resents me most of all. If I can disappear for a while she'll get settled here and then I'll be the outsider—just calling round. We can start from that. She'll feel better then.'

'She'll feel better when somebody tans her hide!' Dora snorted. 'She's seventeen, not seven. Anyhow, I thought you were broke? Where are you going to get away to for this couple of weeks?'

'Greece,' April announced, taking a deep breath and waiting for the horrified speech she knew would be forthcoming. She was not disappointed.

'Greece! You're not falling for that, are you, April? That Greek you met is a playboy and right out of our class. It was all part of the old "catch a girl" game.'

'Pete is very nice,' April assured her seriously. 'I knew him when I was at college. I knew him for a good long time.'

'His name is Petros!' Dora snapped. 'It's no use making him sound safe to my maidenly ears by calling him Pete. I met him, don't forget. He's called Petros Konstantine and that's as Greek as they come—and you know what Greeks are!'

'Just like everybody else—some good, some bad. Pete is one of the good ones. He was great fun and was never more than a friend. I'd like to go out to the island where he lives. To set your suspicious mind at rest, Pete didn't invite me. His mother invited me. I'll not be alone. His whole family are there, including a forbidding older brother apparently. It's just a holiday offered by a nice young man's mother. She means it because she sent me a ticket.'

'One-way, I bet! There's a plot!'

'Return. I live with his family and fly back safely after two weeks.'

'They might hate you, April.' Dora looked at her in astonishment. Adventure was not in Dora's genes and she frequently stared aghast at April.

'His mother is gentle, he told me that, and she sounds it from her letter. His sister Marika is full of fun. As far as I can see, the only fly in the ointment is the older brother, and he's too busy to be out on the island. He lives on the mainland when he's in Greece.'

'It's all lies, you know, April,' Dora assured her anxiously. 'You'll disappear without a trace. You'll get overpowered.'

'I'll get brown,' April laughed, beginning to clear up. 'I'm going at the weekend and I'm staying two weeks. I'll send you a postcard.'

'What's your mum going to say?'

'She knows all about it. I let her read the letter. I'll be gone when she gets back from her honeymoon and then they can settle in without me around under their feet.'

'I bet she's scared for you,' Dora surmised in a horrified voice.

'You know Mum better than that,' April laughed. 'She doesn't get scared; she acts immediately. She rang up Madame Konstantine just to be on the safe side. She was ringing to thank her on the face of it, but actually I've never seen her listening so intently. She was satisfied.'

'Well, I still think it's dangerous.' Dora looked at her steadily. 'You're doing this for Gail, aren't you? You're stepping clear of your own home and going to strangers to let that girl get her foot in.'

'I suppose I am, in a way,' April confessed.

'Oh, April! It's a big mistake. You don't know anything about them and even if Petros was nice here he might be quite different in his home background. You don't even know the others.'

It might be a big mistake, April thought later as she settled for bed at her own small flat, but she felt like doing it. Petros Konstantine had been in England at a college close to her own three years ago, and she had really liked him. A whole gang of them had gone about together and she still kept in touch with the rest of them. For a while she and Petros had written to each other but it had drifted away finally as many friendships did. She remembered him, though. His sunny smile and his sense of humour had appealed to her.

April was an interior designer and worked freelance. Most of the shops recommended her, and for a while things had been going very well. Every house she did had been a spectacular success and her name had been passed on at cocktail parties and coffee mornings. Now, though, even the well-off were being hit by recession and the thought of having the house done over was the last thing they had in mind.

Going away would give her time to think, give her mother time to let Gail know she was welcome, and as far as April could see there was no danger. She had been invited by Madame Konstantine. In any case, she trusted Petros. He had talked endlessly about his home, the small island where his family lived, and as he had talked April had seen in her imagination the sunny island, the blue-green sea, the white houses with coloured roofs. He had laughed at her expression and asked her to visit his house, but she had thought nothing more about it until that letter had come.

There was one thing she had not told Dora, however. In the same post she had received a letter from Petros.

> My family are longing to meet the girl who was so kind to me in England. Please accept the ticket my mother sends as a gift to repay your kindness. Come to visit us and have a nice relaxing holiday. Actually, I need a little help and I know you are game for anything. If you feel embarrassed about having a free holiday, you can rest assured that I need you. It is a little secret that I will disclose when you arrive.

April couldn't see anything wrong with it. Dora always saw disaster in anything. What was wrong with going out to Greece to visit a friend, especially a friend who needed help? At the back of her mind, caution held up a staying hand, but she ignored it.

The invitation had come at just the right time, because things were beginning to get tough. She might well have to re-think her career if things didn't improve, and there was no getting away from it. Her mother had married again after years of being a widow and her new stepfather had a daughter who hated everyone, herself most of all.

Gail Burton resented this marriage, even though her mother had left them a long time ago. She resented the loss of her own beautiful home and she clung ferociously to her father. He was *hers*! Her every action said so, and on the few occasions when they had met as a prospective family she had hardly spoken.

'Give her a while, April,' Cynthia Stewart had said. 'She'll come round.'

Well, a while had passed. Her mother was on an extended honeymoon. Her name was now Burton. Gail glowered at the wedding and wept as they left for Spain. Clearly she had wanted to go too and she had shrugged off April's gentle hand and gone to stay with friends. It was going to spoil her mother's new happiness. A resentful teenager could be very difficult.

April knew she would have to keep away completely for a while to let Gail settle in. Things would be bad enough without the daughter of the house popping in every day. If she didn't come her mother would be hurt. If she came, Gail would feel an outsider. With the house refurbished it would seem like a new place to Gail and maybe she would improve.

The holiday was a godsend because April could never have afforded one herself and it was the perfect excuse to give them time alone to sort out their difficulties, to let Gail feel that the new-look house was her own home and not April's. She had spent a lot of time and money on Gail's room, money she could ill afford, but she wanted a happy family around her. Dora's misgivings would just have to be pushed to the back of her mind.

She had few misgivings as she stepped off the plane at Athens and walked to the arrivals lounge. It was exciting. There wasn't much that April feared. Outside the sun was shining. There was a feeling of adventure in the air and she looked around expectantly. Soon she would see Petros and he would grin in his happy way. She looked at the sea of faces, people waiting to greet friends and relatives. Everybody looked happy.

In England, Petros had been noticeable, tall, very dark and definitely Greek-looking. Here, finding him was a bit difficult. Everybody seemed to be tall, dark and

Greek-looking. It brought a little smile to her lips because she was sure he would find her. It was merely a matter of patience, and she had plenty of that.

There was a man standing at the front and April suddenly found herself reading her own name. He was holding a card up with her name printed in black. 'Miss Stewart'. That really made her smile. It was just like Petros. He would probably be hiding round the corner. She walked forward, her smile growing, too amused to notice the admiring looks she was getting from the men who passed. At any moment Petros would spring out at her. He didn't have any patience at all.

Neither did the man who stood at the back of the crowd. It had been clear that this was the English girl even before she had moved towards the card. Nobody else even remotely like her had come from the plane. He frowned, his hands clenching in annoyance. She was not what he had expected, but then poison could come in a beautiful package and she had willingly played along with Petros.

She didn't look greedy. There was an innocent look about her. Her eyes were astonishingly grey and clear, and he knew that if they mirrored her soul they deceived. She didn't look like a businesswoman and he assumed that Petros had lied about that too. She looked little more than a girl, her figure very slender, her hair a cloudy brown, sweeping her shoulders.

At the side of the women he knew, her skin was amazing—fine, pale, with just a tint of peach. He could see that she wore little make-up, and his lips tightened. Innocence taken to its limit, just a touch of lipgloss on a soft, perfect mouth. She was clever, but perhaps she had overdone the virginal bit. She could hardly pretend to be a schoolgirl, not after the way she had carried on with Petros.

Well, she had plenty of nerve, he could give her credit for that, and his eyes narrowed as she stopped and looked at the man who had held the card for him. She would need plenty of nerve, he thought with satisfaction, and she was soon going to realise that. He walked forward, so tall, so powerful, so impervious to others that people just stepped aside, even those who didn't know him.

He heard his name murmured once or twice.

'Konstantine!' It did not amuse him. He had enough to do without this odious task, and for once he was alone. He would have preferred to move unnoticed, but nobody could act for him and this was not going to be spread around and reach the island. As far as Petros was concerned, this girl had not arrived and he would certainly not see her again. Rumour was not needed. What he had to do he would do alone.

April saw him as he came towards her and shivers of apprehension ran over her skin immediately. Dora's words came rushing back into her mind and she tore her eyes away from the tall, dark man who came purposefully forward. She wished Petros would hurry because this man was coming towards her with a sort of ruthless determination and he had not once taken his eyes from her. If she was going to be overpowered and disappear without trace then it was going to be now.

The man with the card had vanished without her realising it. The fact brought fresh alarm because the tall, intimidating man was now almost up to her. She looked back again to check, hoping he had vanished too, but he was there, right in front of her, and she had to look up a long way to meet his eyes. They were quite black, like jet, still and penetrating in a tanned face that seemed to have been carved from rock. He was handsome in an altogether frightening sort of way, like a statue come to life.

April stared at him, mesmerised, and when he spoke she jumped nervously. It was no use telling herself that there were plenty of people around. This man looked punishingly intent, and the word punishing rang ominously in her mind. He didn't know her but he disliked her and she felt every alarm bell ringing loudly.

'Miss Stewart?' His voice was like steel in black velvet—dark, hard and unyielding.

'Yes.' She looked round anxiously for the man with the card. Petros had sent that man, but where was Petros now? This was taking a joke too far.

'Will you come with me, please?' The Greek statue was speaking to her again, and she glanced at him before hastily looking away, searching the crowd as if her life depended on it. It might do! She wasn't moving from this spot.

'No, thank you. I'm being met.' It should be enough to put him off, although she had to admit he didn't look at all like the sort of man who would accost anyone. He looked wealthy for one thing. She had watched him walk towards her even though she had been a little hypnotised, and she hadn't failed to notice the way other people were looking at him. It might have been with respect, then again it might have been fear.

'*I* am meeting you, Miss Stewart. I see you have your luggage already.'

She had two small cases in her hands and the bigger one at her feet. He reached over to get them, but April was a little too fast for him. She gripped the cases tightly and quickly stepped astride the big case, holding it between her ankles and lifting her head to glare at him.

'Will you please go away? I'm being met by a friend and I don't need any sort of assistance.'

'You were expecting my brother to meet you, *despinis*. Unfortunately he has been detained. I offered to collect you and take you to the island.'

'You're Pete's brother?' She could hardly believe it. They were not at all alike. Petros was smiling, happy, kind, and his build was almost slight for a man. This man was tall and powerful, lean-hipped, broad-shouldered and there was nothing kindly about him. He was all hard masculinity with not a smile in sight.

'I am Michalis Konstantine, Miss Stewart, and I would be grateful if you could bring yourself to accept the fact. I have neither the time nor the inclination to stand about in a crowded airport. My car is outside.'

'Who was the man with the board?' April asked suspiciously.

'A porter. I had to identify you.' He looked down at her in some exasperation. 'As it turned out, you seem to be unique. You certainly do not look Greek. Do you think we could go now?'

Even though Petros had told her about his brother she realised now that he had not said too much. She had only noted the awe. Maybe Greeks were all in awe of their big brothers? This man could have seen her go to the man with the board, though, and her name had been quite clear. Dora's warnings about disappearing were right at the top of her mind.

'Do you have any identification?' she asked with shaky dignity. It earned her a look of utter disbelief and then before she could recover he had grasped a passing porter with one powerful hand and spun him round.

'Is your English good?' he grated.

'Yes, *kyrie*.'

'Then tell me who I am.'

'You—you are Kyrios Konstantine,' the man stammered, wildly. 'You are head of the Konstantine Shipping Line. You are...'

'That will do. I know everything else about myself.' He let the man go and ignored the dazed look of disbelief he received. 'Is that enough, *despinis*, or would you like further testimonials? If you wish I can gather together a Greek chorus who will speak in unison.'

April blushed softly. She wasn't embarrassed, though. It was annoyance. Here was a high-handed Greek and no mistaking it. She was annoyed with Petros too. He had never mentioned any shipping line. According to him they were just a nice, happy family, comfortably off. From the way this man had grabbed the porter and scared him to death she could see that he was quite used to many quaking underlings.

'I'll come with you,' April said quietly. 'I expected Pete to meet me. Surely you realise that I had to be careful?'

'I am sure that you are always careful, Miss Stewart,' he murmured sardonically. He collected her small cases, enclosing them both in one hand as if they weighed nothing at all. As to the big case, he simply snapped his fingers and another awe-stricken porter picked it up and trotted behind them. Apparently he needed his free hand to deal with her. It closed around her arm like a steel clamp, bringing back all the initial fear.

'Will we be joining Pete soon?' she asked a little breathlessly as he hurried her out of the building. Suspicion was still pounding around in her head, but he seemed to be genuine, terrifyingly genuine.

'I hope I have not made an embarrassing mistake, *despinis*,' he grated. 'My brother is called Petros. Can we be speaking of the same person?'

'I called him Pete in England. He said it was more friendly.' His sarcasm was beginning to annoy her very much and she longed to wrench her arm from that hard grasp.

'I'm sure it was,' he muttered, half to himself. 'My brother is extremely friendly.' Which was more than *he* was, April thought angrily. If this was a sample of the Konstantine family she would be using the second half of her ticket tomorrow.

The car was right outside as he had said, and she was grateful to be able to get in and escape the punishing grip. It was the sort of luxurious car a man like that would have, but nothing at all as she had imagined. Petros had had a small sports car when he was in England and he had looked so much at home in it that she had expected to be met with him driving a similar vehicle. This was a Mercedes of the enormous variety. She just sank right into it and it never even stirred when he came and settled behind the wheel.

One secret glance at his tight face had her looking at the airport again with a certain amount of longing. Suppose they were all like this? Suppose Petros was some kind of family freak, the only one with any humanity? She knew that big brother laid down the rules. Petros had told her that laughingly, though. She couldn't find anything to laugh at now.

Petros had also told her that his brother ran the family business and that he himself was a sort of slave sent hither and thither. Now *that* she could believe! And some business! She hadn't even bothered to wonder what it was and, even if she had, shipping would not have entered her mind. She would have been very impressed if they had owned a small fishing boat.

'How far is it to the island?' She made her voice sound cold. If he thought he was scaring her he could just think again. However scared she got, this imperious man was not going to know.

'Some distance,' he said tersely. 'First we need to get to the sea.'

'I'm well aware that islands are surrounded by water!' April snapped. 'I know several geographical facts. I can describe a peninsula.'

'Please do not. Save that for some evening when we are bored,' he said caustically. 'It would be unwise to use up all our conversation in one go.'

She looked at him maliciously. There would be no conversation with this man. As soon as she got to the island she would ignore him, and if it proved to be difficult she would just have to go home because she knew right now that she would never be able to get on with Michalis Konstantine. She lapsed into fuming silence and he simply drove with a grim determination that told her he was utterly unwilling to do this favour for his brother.

April cast a surreptitious look at his hands and was surprised to find them long-fingered and graceful. They handled the wheel with skilful ease and her eyes slid to his wrists, strong, brown, a gold watch glittering just beneath his sleeve, and she didn't need any evidence to prove that he was wealthy. She was still summing him up when he glanced across at her.

'What is your first name?'

'Surely Petros told you?'

'If he did then I was not listening. Disembodied names mean very little. I am to go on calling you Miss Stewart?' He said it in a way that told he imagined that she would insist, in a sort of uneducated way, and it made her voice sharp.

'April.'

'That is your name? April?' There was a suddenly intrigued sound to his voice. 'It is a month in spring. You were born then?'

'I was born in December. My mother was probably tired of the snow.' She felt pleased with her own sarcasm but he ignored it.

'How old are you?'

'Twenty-four. You don't seem to know a lot about me, Mr Konstantine.'

'I do not. I am rarely at home and I missed it all. You have a business of your own, do you not?'

'Not for long, I imagine,' April muttered thought-lessly. 'People are not wanting their houses re-decorating at the moment.'

'So. You paint other people's houses?' he enquired scathingly.

'We can't all run a shipping line, Mr Konstantine. I do what I do best. I'm not afraid of heights.'

'Perhaps you wish to climb higher?' he murmured tightly. April stiffened and turned to face him, bristling with annoyance.

'Just what do you mean by that? I hope you're not suggesting that I came here with any ulterior motive in mind?'

'Why should I imagine that, Miss Stewart? All I know is that you are a friend of my brother and he has per-suaded my mother to send you a ticket to visit him on the island. I understand that he enjoyed your warm company in England.'

She didn't need any more spelling out to her. His tone was enough. He thought she and Petros were lovers and he was fetching her out here because of that. April blushed hotly. Did his mother think that? How had they got the idea? Petros had never even thought of it, and he would have been dropped rapidly if he had. She kept silent. It was nothing to do with this man. She didn't know him and already she hated him. Maybe she should have stayed behind and given Gail a good talking-to instead of coming out here?

Every bit of pleasure had gone out of it, and she wished heartily that she had turned and run when she saw Michalis Konstantine. The thought had certainly been there. She was probably going to be introduced to a high-powered family who would regard her with suspicion and contempt.

'Pete is just a friend,' she said desperately.

'I am sure he is. No doubt he will be a friend still—when you see him.'

They drove on in silence. Athens was left behind without her even noticing and it was only when the journey seemed to be stretching on and on that April became alarmed again. She had only hazy ideas as to where they were and she did not even know if they had turned north or south. There were so many islands that the place where Petros lived could have been off any coast. She never asked.

'It's getting dark,' she finally ventured uneasily.

'The sun goes down all over the world. You did not take an early flight.'

'I had too much to do,' she murmured. She had been back to the house and given everything a last-minute polish. She had been obliged to take a later flight than she had wished. 'All the same, I never expected such a long journey. Will we get to the island before dark?'

'I think not. It does not matter, surely? You will see Petros in the lamplight—more romantic.'

It silenced April very effectively. She was *not* going to start protesting and explaining herself to this arrogant Greek. She would let Petros do it, and she would stand there and smile in a superior manner. Michalis Konstantine would have to face embarrassment then and she would just love it!

The country became wilder and more deserted but after a while her hopes rose again. She could smell the sea. Soon she could even hear it. There was a mixture of tantalising smells drifting through the open windows of the car—wild herbs and pine. She identified them and peered into the gathering gloom. There were mountains not too far away and soon they were running on a road that seemed to be skirting cliffs. It didn't worry her. Maybe this was where the ferry to the island docked? Maybe Michalis Konstantine owned the ferry?

The road suddenly stopped quite abruptly and in the headlights she could see tall iron gates set in a high stone wall. Even then she had no inclination of any danger, not even when he pressed a button on the dashboard and the gates swung open obediently. She looked behind as they passed and saw the gates close behind them. She heard them too. The sound was very definite, final.

The road was now little more than the drive to some big house and she had been quite right about the smell of pine. There were pine woods at each side of the road, dark and mysterious in the headlights. Nerves came rushing back and she found her hands clenching together. Frantically she ran over the meeting and the words he had said, but she could not fault her own logic. That porter had definitely said that this was Konstantine— unless he had been paid to say it?

'Where are we?' She could not keep silent any longer and she knew her voice was scared.

'Almost there,' he assured her smoothly. 'Round the next bend you will see the house.'

'The house? What about the island? Is Petros at this house?'

'He is not, Miss Stewart. This is my house.' The sound of his voice was now menacing, and April turned to look at him closely. What she saw did not make her feel any better. He looked very grim indeed and very satisfied with himself.

'Do—do we have to stay here until daylight?' she asked hopefully.

'Most assuredly,' he rasped.

They rounded the bend and she could see the house, tall and white, gardens around it that sloped to the edge of the cliff. The lights were on, including some around the outside. It meant they would not be alone even if Petros had not arrived yet. Somebody had put those lights on, because it had been daylight when he had met her at the airport.

The mountains now seemed closer as if they had moved to encircle the house—mountains, pine woods and the cliff that led to the sea. She felt endangered but she held tightly to common sense. He was not a bandit. He was Michalis Konstantine. The name was right. This tight feeling was probably just her dislike of him.

'Will Petros be coming?' she asked.

'He is on the island and he will stay there if he knows what is good for him,' the deep voice said coldly.

'But what about tomorrow? Are you taking me out to the island tomorrow? You said we had to stay here until daylight and I can understand that but...'

'And many daylights to come, Miss Stewart,' he said harshly.

'I—I don't know what you mean.'

'Then I will explain, *despinis*. You are not going to any island. You are not meeting my brother. I have brought you to my house. It is miles from anywhere, safe, secluded, impregnable. My way of life requires security, and here I have it. The house is isolated, hidden even. Few know of its existence. You are here until I decide to let you leave and any attempt to escape will be useless. There is only one way out—the path to the gate. The wall has electric alarms. The gate has the same. Your other choice would be to climb down the cliff and swim but, I warn you, it is a long way to Athens.'

'You can't mean this! Why are you doing it?' April whispered. Her hands were beginning to shake and she clenched them more tightly.

'I am doing this because my brother has got himself mixed up with an adventuress. He is a Konstantine. His marriage is arranged. You will not interfere because you will be here with me. You will never see Petros again. There is no way that I will simply put you back on to a flight to England and leave you free to communicate with him. As far as he is concerned, you did not arrive, you were merely playing him along. I am responsible for my family, and no greedy young woman is going to destroy carefully laid plans by sinking her claws into my brother. You will stay here until he is safely engaged and committed to marriage. I assure you, he will soon forget all about you.'

CHAPTER TWO

MICHALIS pulled up in front of the house, grimly satisfied with his speech, and as soon as he stopped the car April leapt out and ran. She could hardly believe that this was happening to her, and she had no idea how he had got such crazy ideas about her and Petros. For all she knew he was a rich lunatic, and she was not about to take any chances. She had never been as scared as this in her life, but she could take care of herself and she could run like the wind.

April ran fast but after a few yards certain hard facts penetrated her brain. She knew they were isolated—he had not needed to point that out to her. It must have been ages since they had passed any sort of civilisation. Out of the circle of the house lights and the headlights of the car it was pitch-black. She may well be able to run but she could not run back to Athens. He had locked the gates for one thing and it was too dark to even find the gates at the moment.

She had jumped out and run without her bag too. Her return ticket, her passport and the little money she had were all in that bag and the cases contained her very best things. She stopped and turned round, disheartened to see that in fact she had not run very far at all. She could see Michalis Konstantine, and he was ignoring her. He was lifting her suitcases from the car and putting them on the steps that led to the house.

As she watched, the front door opened and a man came out. He looked old. Whatever age he was he was not a young, vigorous man, threatening and powerful. She would get help. This could not be some sort of conspiracy. Petros didn't know about it for one thing. She was just faced with dealing with one power-mad lunatic. Anyone else would be shocked.

She ran back with the same speed, and Michalis never even turned his head. It infuriated her because he was obviously so arrogantly sure of his captive that he had behaved as if she were still sitting in the car, and he didn't seem to care who knew she was here. He merely slanted her an ironically amused look and went on speaking to the man. April interrupted breathlessly.

'Help me! Oh, please help! This man has kidnapped me!'

She planted herself in front of the older man and appealed to him urgently, looking up into his face and showing great agitation, fully expecting to see a shocked reaction. He just looked at her blankly and when Michalis spoke to him in Greek he nodded and walked off into the house, taking the cases and ignoring her except for a very slight smile that contained a certain amount of astonishment.

'Georgios speaks only Greek, *despinis*. As an ally he will be of little use unless you care to draw him a series of pictures. Even that will now be looked upon as normal with you, I fear.'

Michalis Konstantine's dark voice showed his amusement and he looked down at her with a sardonic smile. April glared up at him.

'What have you just said to him?' she demanded heatedly.

'He was naturally surprised at your vehemence. I told him that you were asking for a cup of tea. I explained that the English become rather desperate about such things.'

She could see why she had got that odd look from Georgios. Petros had a very ruthless and clever brother. With a few words he had branded her as mad.

'Don't think you're going to get away with this!' she raged. 'You can't keep me here. As soon as it's daylight I'll be off like a shot.'

'At least you have the sense to realise that escape attempts are useless at night,' he murmured silkily. 'I had visions of finding you exhausted and bedraggled in the woods at dawn.'

That told her a lot too. He would go to bed and sleep peacefully knowing a defenceless woman was all alone and scared in the night. He was a cruel tyrant and completely without scruples.

'I came back because I left my handbag behind,' she said haughtily. 'As soon as it's daylight I'll be off again, and don't imagine your stupid gates are going to stop me. I can climb like a cat!'

'Surely it is "like a monkey"? Let us go in, Miss Stewart. If you are to begin your race to Athens tomorrow you need all the sleep you can get.' He handed her her bag politely and she snatched it from him, turning to the house before that steel-like hand could grasp her arm again.

'I agree with you. I would now like that cup of tea if you don't mind.' Another thought had occurred to April. She wondered if Georgios had a wife. If he did, and if they both lived here then maybe the woman spoke English.

'Georgios is already preparing tea, Miss Stewart. He will take your luggage to your room later. You can then unpack before dinner. Sofia will serve it when we are ready.'

A little smile flickered around April's stubborn lips and he looked down at her with the same caustic amusement.

'When the meal is over it will be polite to say *ef-charistó* to Sofia. She does not speak English either.'

April's smile flickered out and she stepped into the lighted hall with a very grim expression on her face. So he had thought of everything? Not quite! For one thing he didn't know that she was more angry than scared. He didn't know that she had never lost a battle in her life. She could climb, she could swim and she was going to get out of here as soon as it was light. She would go straight to the police.

No, she wouldn't. He was too well-known, too rich, too powerful. For all she knew, the police might not speak English either and he would come along with some plausible tale that would have them locking her up for her own safety. That would please Michalis Konstantine because she would be safely out of the way then too. She would go to the British Embassy, show her passport, tell her tale and get back to England. She would then write to the papers.

The thought gave her an enormous feeling of superiority until she thought of her mother. She was supposed to be safely with Madame Konstantine. Her mother had problems enough without feelings of guilt that she had not checked things out thoroughly, and April knew her mother well—she always blamed herself.

Things were getting more tricky by the minute. It looked as if she would have to get herself out of here and back to England with no help at all. She was so deep

in thought that she just kept on walking, and the hand
came to her arm with the same hard grip.

'Let us take tea in the *sala*, Miss Stewart. I very much
doubt if Georgios will have served it in the kitchen.'

He turned her round and headed her towards an open
door, and it was only then that April found herself
shaking with reaction. So far she had been scared, angry
and enraged. She had run as fast as possible and then
run back, she had argued and seethed, but now she was
exhausted with it all. Her legs were shaking and all she
wanted to do was sit down and imagine it was a
nightmare. When he pointed her in the direction of a
beautiful, brocade-covered settee, she almost collapsed
into it.

The room was fabulous. She hadn't even considered
what it would be like in this house because she had never
had any intention of being inside it. Now that she was
resting her shaking legs she could see that the room was
expertly done and it seemed to be filled with treasures.
No wonder he had alarms all over the gates and walls.
He seemed to have robbed an art gallery, but most likely
he had bought one and simply removed the contents!

The walls were white and a perfect setting for the gold-
framed pictures. She recognised two Corots, a Degas, a
Manet and over the fireplace was a Canaletto. The whole
room was a mixture of tastes and, unbelievably, everything went together superbly, making it a rich but
comfortable room. In different circumstances she would
have loved staying here just for this room alone.

The floors were polished wood, the effect softened by
several Chinese rugs, and April had wild visions of him
giving orders to his skippers to bring back plunder from
foreign parts. There was a black Chinese cabinet in one
corner with snowy white cranes on each door, and she

was just beginning to make a rough estimate of the cost of putting together this room when Georgios came in with the tea.

He smiled at her soothingly and she noticed he placed the tray very close to her. No doubt he imagined she would spring on it if he put it even a foot away. She was branded as a desperate tea-drinker and he wouldn't be likely to forget it. Help in that direction was doubtful and, in any case, he was a slave of the master.

April didn't want to disappoint him so she started to pour immediately, but her hands were shaking so much that she had to stop almost at once and, as the door closed softly behind Georgios, Michalis spoke in that dark, worrying voice.

'You are safe, *despinis*. Nothing unpleasant is about to happen to you.'

'It's already happened,' April reminded him shakily.

'You are a captive, I admit, but, putting that aside, you will be well looked after. You will be fed and cared for. The house is isolated but very luxurious.'

'You can't dismiss kidnapping in that offhand way,' April informed him indignantly. 'It can't be "put aside". It's a criminal offence and you'll not get away with it!'

'I will get away with it for the time that is necessary. Petros is about to become engaged. When he realises that you are no longer interested he will come to his senses and proceed with the engagement. After that, matters will take their course.'

'You mean, matters will take *your* course! I've never met anyone like you in my whole life. You've kidnapped me and it's obvious that you're forcing your brother into a marriage he does not want.'

'How do you know that, Miss Stewart? Your know-ledge of my family consists of nights of passion with my brother in England. I know Petros. He will have told you precisely what he wished you to know and nothing else. I would imagine that your pillow talk was somewhat stilted.'

April blushed rose-pink. The only head next to hers on a pillow was her old, shabby teddy-bear. Michalis Konstantine was talking to her as if she were a well-known seductress.

'I realise that you're making this up as you go along,' she said hotly. 'Obviously you're drawing on your own experiences to fill in the details. Petros and I were simply friends.'

He looked at her disdainfully and she could see that even talking about it was making his temper rise, so she tried a new tack.

'It's quite clear to me that you're wealthy,' she pointed out coldly. 'It's also obvious that it's gone to your head. Let me tell you, though, that being rich will not allow you to get away with kidnapping. Petros may be fooled into thinking I never arrived, but I have a family in England. I didn't suddenly spring out of a parcel. People will want to know where I am. The police will look for me.'

'Why should they? You are on holiday with a friend. Did you tell your family the name of the island?'

'*Yes*!' She hoped there wouldn't be a written test because she had been trying to remember the name of the island for ages. She wasn't even sure that Petros had told her, come to think of it. A little of her confusion must have shown because he leaned back in his seat and pinned her with those cold black eyes.

'Then tell me, *despinis*.' When she didn't answer he smiled that nasty, sardonic smile again and looked extremely self-satisfied. 'Greece is surrounded by islands.

The island in question is private. It belongs to my family. By the time these mythical police have searched the well-known islands, Petros will be safely engaged and you will be back in your own country.'

'Your mother will want to know why I haven't arrived,' April informed him triumphantly. 'She can easily find out that my ticket has been used.'

'She will be told that you decided simply to stay in Athens. It will be an insulting gesture but she will survive the insult.'

'My family won't believe that,' April snapped. 'They'll be expecting to hear from me. I always send postcards.'

'They will not be unduly alarmed. After all, you are supposedly on an island far from civilisation. They will imagine that the post is almost non-existent. Before they become worried I will have you safely back with them.'

He nodded to the tea. 'Pour your tea. I do not want Georgios thinking that he is incapable of meeting your anxious demands. As he will be helping Sofia to look after you during your stay, it would undermine his self-confidence.'

April made another attempt to get her drink but her hands seemed to be shaking even more now, and he suddenly got up and came towards her, alarming her instantly until she found that he intended to pour the tea himself. He just crouched down by the table and steadily poured the hot tea, carefully adding milk and then putting it close to her hand.

It was an unexpectedly kind action and quite startled her. At close hand he was disturbingly attractive. His hair gleamed in the lights, his lashes as he looked down at his task were thick and curled, and he was wearing some tangy aftershave that pleased her nostrils. It somehow gave her courage. Maybe he wasn't so bad? If she explained it all...

'You can't really believe that Pete and I were anything but friends,' she began quietly. 'I only knew him for a little while really and...'

'That is supposed to excuse you?' His head shot up and those dark eyes narrowed with anger. 'Petros is a perfectly normal male. With looks like yours I would imagine it was easy to lure him immediately—the first night you met!'

'If that were true, doesn't it make him equally guilty? Why am I taking all the blame?'

She knew she was saying exactly the wrong thing, and his eyes sparked with further anger, but there was this chauvinistic attitude that made her the wicked woman and his brother a poor little thing. If this had all been true she would still have been the one to be blamed.

'I do not excuse him!' he grated, standing and glaring down at her. 'He knows my anger and will continue to feel it. However, he is my brother. You are nothing.'

'Thank you,' April said bitterly, pushing her tea aside and standing as he moved impatiently away from her. 'You're entitled to your opinion, of course, but, as it happens, you're wrong. Far from being nothing, I'm now quite important. I'm a kidnap victim and *you* are going to be quite notorious when I get out of here.'

'That is in the future,' he reminded her scathingly.

'It's tomorrow morning,' she snapped. 'Call your serf. I want to go to my room—unless you're locking me in the cellar?'

'You will be comfortable. I have told you,' he rasped, standing across the room and fixing her with a very baleful eye.

'I'll be a prisoner,' April reminded him. '*You* are a criminal. Of course you probably always were but, be that as it may, you're certainly one now. When I get out of here you'll be on the front page of every newspaper in England.' There was no need for him to know that she wouldn't do that. It was time he had a few worries in his lofty world.

'They will not be at all interested,' he surmised scathingly. 'Women like you are not news.'

'Shipping magnates are! The bigger they come, the harder they fall!' April lifted her chin proudly and walked out of the room. If Georgios didn't appear she would search the house to see where he had put her cases. The next time she saw Michalis Konstantine it would be on a 'wanted' poster!

She saw him immediately because he came with her, and when she turned to glare at him he looked down at her with ill-contained impatience.

'I am not about to murder you, Miss Stewart! Georgios will now be helping with dinner. I will show you to your room.'

She loathed the way he imagined he could mix his criminal ways with politeness. Here he was again behaving in much the same way he had behaved when he had poured her tea: the careful host. Any onlooker would have imagined she was here willingly.

She walked silently up the stairs, noting more wonderful works of art lining the curved flight of steps. The stairs were carpeted. She would be able to creep down here early in the morning. Her satisfaction at this was rather subdued because she was very much aware of Michalis walking behind her. The back of her neck was tingling as if he was watching her closely and she hoped he couldn't hear her thoughts. She had announced her intentions but he probably didn't believe her. He would find out!

April had to make a great effort not to gasp with pleasure as she stepped into the bedroom when he opened the door for her. It was softly lamp-lit, the whole room a subtle mixture of peach and blue, softest shades that were picked up by the covers on the bed and the long silken curtains. Her feet seemed to sink into the carpet and for a second she just stood still, almost in awe. The very simplicity spoke of wealth. As a bedroom it was just about perfect.

'Your bathroom is through here,' he said coldly as she just stood there without speaking. He flung another door open and she caught a glimpse of a gleaming bathroom before he closed the door again. 'Dinner will be served in half an hour.'

He started to walk out but April felt the need to have the last word.

'I shall stay here. I'm not about to pretend to be an honoured guest.'

'You are a guest even though you are most certainly not honoured,' he bit out. 'I shall expect to see you at dinner. While you are here you will be treated carefully. The only reason you are here is to keep you away from my brother. The care that will be extended to you does not include room service. Sofia and Georgios are not young and they will not serve your meals here in this room.'

'I don't want a meal!' April snapped. 'I'd rather starve than eat with you.'

'You will not starve, *despinis*,' he assured her icily. 'You will present yourself at the table whenever a meal is ready. Having you here is unpleasant enough without further problems.'

He walked out and shut the door and April stared after him angrily. What did he propose to do if she chose to remain in her room—drag her to the table by her hair? She had no intention of eating with him. She wasn't about to make this captivity anything he could congratulate himself on later. If she wasn't careful, he would be able to tell people she had come willingly and had a very nice holiday.

April made no attempt to unpack. She wasn't staying after all. She found her nightie and toiletries and left everything else where it was. There was no chance of taking her cases when she escaped but she would get them later—with a police escort.

She walked to the window and looked out. Even with the window closed she could hear the sound of the sea. She had heard it since they had come into the room and when she opened the window she was not disappointed. The moon was now up and the sea lay before her like a silver and black plain, moonlight rippling across the waves. There was a small balcony with white wrought-iron table and chairs, and she stepped outside and looked down.

She was at the front of the house. She could see the car they had arrived in, and for a moment the idea of climbing down and stealing it came to her mind. She discarded the thought. He had probably taken the keys and, even if he had not, she knew the sound of the engine would alert him. He would most likely have some device in the house for keeping those huge gates locked. No, it would have to be under her own steam.

The garden sloped down to the edge of the cliffs, the sea beyond it. From here at this time of night it was impossible to tell how high the cliffs were or even if there was any beach at all. It seemed an unlikely avenue of escape. The woods looked more promising and she leaned out to have a closer look.

A door downstairs opened and she drew back quickly as Michalis stepped out and walked to the low balustrade that edged the front of the house. If he looked up he would see her silhouetted against the bedroom lights, but she doubted if he would look up. He seemed to be brooding and she assumed it was about her. He stood with his hands in his pockets and looked out towards the sea. Everything about him bristled with anger and she was just about to go back to her room when he suddenly ran his hand through his hair and then turned on his heel and walked back into the house.

He was frustrated. What had he expected after all— a nice willing captive? His frustration amused her. It also changed her mind about dinner. With a bit of luck she could drive him mad. She was hungry too and thirsty after she had haughtily walked away from that tea. She decided to get ready and then go down. Some good might come of it. If she couldn't drive him mad she might be able to make him see how idiotic this was. In any case, it was no use contemplating escape if she was frantically hungry.

She was still wearing her travelling clothes—a lemon blouse and matching skirt—and she looked at herself in the long mirror in the bathroom. Lemon suited her as most colours did; her brown hair, shining and long, seemed to pick up lights from it. She just changed her shoes, putting on high heels. They gave her a feeling of supremacy, and she would need it.

Michalis Konstantine had done nothing but look at her with contempt. She felt more able to look down her

nose at him with the advantage of a little more height—
not that it would make her anywhere near his height.
He was as tall and splendid as the god he resembled. He
was also godlike in his feeling of total superiority. She
would change that.

He showed no surprise when she went down to the
sala. He was having a drink, and got up at once to pour
one for her.

'Sherry, Miss Stewart?'

'A gin and tonic, please.' April didn't even want a
drink but she wanted to keep a mood of optimism. He
was polite as usual, and when almost at once Georgios
appeared to tell them that dinner was ready Michalis indicated that she should take her drink in with her.

This was quite ridiculous. A captive guest. She stole
a look at her powerful host and looked away quickly as
she found his eyes on her thoughtfully.

'You changed your mind about dinner?' he asked.

'I'm hungry. I've never thought it a good idea to
punish myself.' April raised her head and looked back
at him steadily. He didn't look so alarming, here in his
own house. Surely he didn't mean to go through with
this?

'You will enjoy Sofia's cooking.' It was sheer madness,
this civilised conversation from a man who had actually
kidnapped her, and April took a deep breath and tried
her last shot as they sat to eat.

'Look. I've got over my outrage at your behaviour
and I'm prepared to tell you all you want to know about
my friendship with Petros. Do you think we could talk
sensibly?'

'We can make an attempt.' He just went on eating and
never looked up, and April knew it was up to her to

convince him that he was quite mistaken about her character.

'I don't really know your brother very well,' she began carefully. 'When he was at college, my college was close by. Students tend to congregate together and we met. There were always other people with us. It was nothing but friendship. He's very amusing and—and charming. That's all really. He came home to Greece, we wrote to each other a couple of times and then we didn't even bother with that. I never expected to hear from him again.'

'You were quick to accept the invitation. A friend from quite a while ago and out of the blue he wants you with him.' He looked across at her coolly as Georgios came in to serve dessert. So far, April had not even noticed what she had been eating. It was hard to talk evenly when those intent black eyes watched closely.

'It—it was convenient . . .'

'An odd remark.' He leaned forward to pour her some more wine and she was lulled into another confession.

'Well, my mother is marrying again and I wanted to get away for a while.'

'I see.' He didn't see, and she was about to rashly tell him even more when she noticed the look in his eyes. He hadn't believed a word of this. She was wasting her time. April kept silent, finishing her dessert and sipping the wine. She wasn't going to tell him another thing unless he showed some sign of softening his attitude.

'And your exact relationship to my brother?' It was more a command than a question, and she looked up indignantly.

'I've told you! He's a friend. A friend I don't even know very well now.'

For a moment he sat contemplating her silently and she hoped he was turning things over in his mind with a view to letting her go. He surely didn't think she looked like a seductress? There was nothing seductive about her. She was just a girl who worked for her living, not like any of the women *he* would know!

He sat back and looked across at her with the same speculation.

'An interesting story, *despinis*,' he stated. 'Now I will tell you what *I* know. My brother has confessed that he met you at college. You were not, however, simply friends. According to Petros there was instant and mutual attraction. Far from being part of a merry crowd of students, you lived together at your flat for the rest of the time he was in England.'

'I don't believe you!' April said hotly, her eyes wide open. 'Petros would never say anything like that because it's just not true. He's never even been to my flat and, as for two people living there, there's not enough room!'

'He did not confess willingly,' Michalis conceded icily.

'You mean you had to beat it out of him?' April looked at him furiously and she got one of those sardonic smiles that went nowhere near his eyes.

'Threats were sufficient. Petros has a very large allowance as I'm sure you know.'

'He works for what he gets!'

'He appears when the mood takes him and generally manages to complicate every arrangement,' Michalis corrected her. 'When he is married he will toe the line— I believe that is your English expression?'

'Then he was lying to me as skilfully as he's lied to you,' April pointed out. 'He's never been to my flat and we were not—not...'

'Lovers? I believe you were, Miss Stewart. I believe that, for once, Petros has met his match as far as deceit goes. You obviously knew he was wealthy. According to my brother, he invited you here because he cannot bear to be without you any longer, and I can imagine why. You have the sort of innocent beauty that could trap any unwary victim. Fortunately I have been able to stop your plans and you will leave here when I am ready to let you go.'

'You must have some doubts,' April pleaded anxiously. He had just discounted everything she had said and she was shocked at his unbending attitude. She just couldn't believe that Petros had told this fantastic tale.

'If I had any, you have set my mind at rest,' he assured her grimly. 'I am to believe that an innocent young woman would fly out to Greece, to someone she had not seen for a long time, someone who was merely a friend?'

'Yes!' April stormed. 'I can't see anything wrong with it.'

'Which is a pity, *despinis*. With a little more decorum you would not now be a prisoner,' he pointed out smoothly.

'I shan't be for long.'

'You are anxious to get back to your small flat and your failing business venture? You are desperate to see your newly married mother and a stepfather who clearly does not accept you?'

'He does! He's very nice.'

'You are wasting your time, Miss Stewart. I know the truth and I have acted on it. When Petros is safely engaged you may go back to your own peculiar life.'

'The only peculiar thing is you and your insane ideas!' April snapped. 'If all this tale is true then I can only say that, knowing your brother as you obviously imagine you do, you also know he is lying.'

'One of you is lying, clearly,' he admitted. 'I am placing my bets carefully because I cannot see any gain to Petros in lying on this occasion, whereas you, *despinis*, have a lot to gain.'

'Name one thing!'

'A fortune. A share in the Konstantine wealth. You would not be the first to have tried, and I admit too that you are the most innocent-looking. Too bad that it did not work. However, you have visited Greece.'

'I've visited an airport and ended up in a prison,' April pointed out bitterly. 'I can see I've been wasting my time talking to you. Tomorrow I'm leaving, and don't say I haven't warned you about this. Criminals get caught, even wealthy criminals.'

She got up and stormed out of the room, and she was even more irritated when he stood politely and nodded at her in a civilised manner. In the hall she met Sofia, a middle-aged woman with a kindly face, and she began to seek help yet again but all she got was an anxious and uncomprehending smile. There really was no help at all.

April searched her mind and managed to say, '*Efcharistó*.' At least that got her a beaming look, and when she turned she was filled with fury to see Michalis Konstantine standing at the door of the dining-room with a smile of sheer amusement on his face. He could laugh! She would see him in prison before she had finished with him.

CHAPTER THREE

APRIL had planned to be up at dawn, but when she awoke strong sunlight was pouring into the room and Sofia was busily carrying in a tray. It was the opening of the door that had awakened her, and April realised that it must be quite late. A glance at her watch told her it was already seven-thirty, and she felt very annoyed with herself. So much for a dawn escape!

She got a warm smile from Sofia, who put the tray by her bed. It was tea, croissants and a very sticky-looking jam.

'*Efcharistó*.' April remembered her one word of Greek and it earned her a further smile.

'*Parakalo, despinis*.' She left the room, her small figure clothed entirely in black, and April sat up with a sigh. She might as well fill up on this breakfast. It might have to last for a long time and it was a good thing anyway. She wouldn't have to face Michalis Konstantine in the dining-room.

Later when she was showered and dressed she went on the balcony and surveyed the scene. The day was good, not a cloud in sight. The sea was calm and blue and out across the great sweeping bay she could see a boat with white sails tacking smoothly with the slight breeze. It would have been a wonderful place to stay if it hadn't been a prison.

The woods did not look so threatening in daylight, and she could see that if she went just a little way in and skirted the trees she would be able to get to the gates

42

easily and not be spotted from the house. All she had to do was get out into the sunlight and run. She had dressed for action in blue jeans and a white T-shirt, her white trainers on her feet. She picked up a cardigan and her handbag and stealthily let herself out into the passage.

There wasn't a sound. It was so very quiet that she thought that maybe Michalis had gone out somewhere. He was quite likely to do that. He was so sure she was trapped. He hadn't taken the car because she had seen it from her balcony, but that was nothing. He might have six cars round the back for all she knew.

She made it to the lower hall with no difficulty, and she was just about to make a silent run for the front door when she heard his voice. April shrank back against the wall, but she soon realised he was talking on the telephone. He was in another downstairs room, one she had not entered last night, and she imagined it was his study. With a business so great he would not even be able to take time off for kidnapping. He was probably in touch with his office. It gave her the chance she needed and she ran quickly across the shining hall and out into the morning sun.

Her heart was hammering but she reached the trees. They were close to the house at one side and April made for that side and shelter. Once there, she stopped, listening carefully until she was sure that her escape had gone unnoticed. He would probably think she was sulking in her room. Then again, he might imagine that any seductress worth her salt would stay in bed till noon.

She set off through the trees, keeping the drive in sight but also keeping a wary eye out for pursuit, ready to duck down at the slightest sign of danger. Nothing happened at all and she began to grin to herself. How easy!

Michalis Konstantine was not as clever as he thought. She could just imagine his furious face when he found the captive missing.

It proved to be a long way to the gate. In the car it had not seemed so long but on foot it was quite far from the house. She could hear the sea on her right-hand side and all the time she was unconsciously waiting for the sound of other footsteps on the drive. When she at last saw the high wall and the big wrought-iron gates she felt greatly relieved. This escape business was nerve-racking and her day had only just begun.

She risked stepping on to the drive and went to survey the obstacle that stood between her and freedom. The gates were very high, as high as the wall, but their design gave plenty of room for foot-holds. The alarm system was another problem. She began to look the gates over carefully, but try as she might she could not see anything even vaguely resembling an alarm. No switches, no wires, no box.

So much for his security! It was perfectly obvious that he had just said that to scare her, to make her feel that escape was impossible. All these gates were electronically controlled to let cars in and out. Another obstacle dispatched.

April began to climb. It was remarkably easy. Her trainers gripped well and the carved gates gave plenty of hand-holds. As to the height, it didn't bother her now any more than it had ever done. She had her handbag slung like a school satchel over her shoulder, her cardigan tied round her waist, and everything was going well.

The siren began as she reached the halfway mark, and it was so sudden, so deafening that she almost fell with the shock. It screeched through her ears like a mad banshee and it seemed to be coming from everywhere at once. Panic took hold of her and she began to climb faster, wanting both to get to the top before anyone came and wanting to get out of range of the noise.

A hand gripped her ankle and she screeched herself as she was relentlessly pulled downwards.

'Stop it! I'll fall,' April yelled at the top of her voice, looking round and downwards to find Michalis standing there, his hand gripping her cruelly and his expression telling her that if she fell it would be a very good thing and save him a great deal of further trouble.

'Stop it!' He went on exerting pressure and she was now clinging with both hands, her ears threatening to burst with the noise. With his free hand he took a small black box from his pocket and aimed it at the gates, and there was instant blissful silence, so much silence in fact that for a minute April thought she had gone deaf.

'Climb down or I will pull you down,' he threatened severely. Now that her brain was not being bombarded by sound waves she could see that he had brought the car. The noise had been so loud that she had not heard it. Even so, he had been remarkably quick off the mark.

'Make your mind up, Miss Stewart,' he said menacingly. 'I have little patience. Climb down or fall down.'

With her ankle going numb she didn't have a lot of choice, and she began her descent very glumly. Her ears were still ringing and she felt decidedly unsafe; all her balance had gone. When her feet touched the floor her legs just folded beneath her and she sat on the drive, shaking her head to clear it.

'Sound waves can be lethal. Remember that.' He sounded remarkably unconcerned and April looked up at him angrily.

'They're probably illegal! There's no sign that an alarm is fitted. If anyone broke in and got caught up in that they'd be damaged.'

'Therefore be grateful that I saw you leaving the house as I looked through the window of my study. I was able to follow you in the car and keep out of sight. As to the alarm system, the whole gate is alarmed from just under halfway. It is modern technology. In Greece we are not medieval in everything.' He suddenly smiled down at her, infuriatingly amused, and April glared at him.

'You deliberately let me climb and get caught in that— that screeching...' she began furiously.

'I wanted you to know that I was speaking the truth. I wished to forestall any further foolishness. I was waiting to rescue you. Be grateful.'

'You took your time!'

'A lesson, *despinis*, is useless unless it is a good one. Come along. I will take you back to the house.'

He scooped her up with one hand, his arm coming round her waist, and she shuddered at the contact, trying to pull away. It merely amused him further.

'Do not fall down if you do not wish to be picked up. I imagine, though, that it is merely your devious nature. A man's arm around your waist must be very tame to you.'

'I like to choose the man,' April said tartly. 'Never in my blackest nightmares would I choose you.'

'No?' He swung her towards him, his hands coming to her shoulders with frightening strength. 'I am surprised, Miss Stewart,' he murmured. 'You chose Petros and yet my brother is relatively poor until he is thirty. As he is only twenty-six you would have had a long time to wait for wealth and in the meantime I would have been firmly in control of all the money you crave. On the other hand, I am wealthy right now, both in the family business and in my own right. I would have thought myself a better target for so greedy a magpie. How unfortunate that you did not meet me first.'

'I've *told* you——!' April began, but he stared at her cynically and interrupted.

'And I have listened. Your actions have given you away, even this attempt at escape. Any girl with any sense would have simply sat it out, behaved reasonably and had a good holiday in a luxurious house by the sea. If you had been truthful you would have been afraid, upset. I find that you are merely enraged. Of course you cannot afford to wait things out, can you? Petros will be engaged soon and that will be too late for you. I can understand that escape is necessary. However, it is impossible, so be sensible and settle down.'

Settle down! April seethed. It was useless to protest any further and she knew it. Nothing she said or did would convince him of her innocence. She might just as well keep trying because she could never be thought of more savagely than she already was. And she didn't care what he thought anyway. He led her to the car and she sank into the seat with a very bad grace.

He had won the first round but she wasn't finished yet. There were the walls and then there was the sea. On reflection she could understand that the gates could be one great big alarm system. They were metal. The wall was stone. How did you wire a stone wall? As far as she could see, it could not be done. Next stop the wall—this very day if possible.

She decided to bide her time until after lunch. When they got back to the house both Georgios and Sofia were in the hall looking completely mystified. They had heard the alarm but they received no explanation from

Michalis. He simply glanced at his watch and told April that lunch would be served in an hour. It gave her time for action and she used it well.

She put her handbag and cardigan in her room, freshened up a little and then proceeded to do everything she could to get on his nerves. He was back in his study as she went down the stairs but this time he had taken the precaution of leaving the door open. As she passed he frowned at her menacingly, his black brows drawn together and his mouth in one tight line. He disliked her intensely and didn't hesitate to show it, but it was all one to April—the feeling was mutual and *she* had good cause. He simply believed lies. He could hate her as much as he liked.

She sauntered out into the grounds, keeping well away from the side of the house with the study. It was very warm in the sun and she wished this was just a holiday. The house and the setting were beautiful. It was not a holiday, though; she was a prisoner, and he must know some very simpering women if he thought anyone would just settle down to enjoy captivity.

It was a good chance to look at the drop to the sea and April walked across the lawn to the cliff-edge. It was a rocky cliff, not too high but with a few quite horrendous rocks at sea level. Right now the sea lapped them calmly but she had visions of how they would look if the sea became angry. She could easily get down there, though. It would have to be in daylight, but it was possible. Just to the side a small beach started, and leaning over she could see that it stretched out of sight and in the right direction.

She would try the wall first, though. When she turned round she saw Michalis watching her from the window of the *sala*, his black frown intact, and she had to work very hard not to smile triumphantly. If he thought he could calmly get on with his business while she sat about languidly he could think again. If he wanted to be sure where she was he would have to follow.

And follow he did. She wandered around in each direction from the house, partly to assess the lie of the land but mainly to have him chasing all over to keep an eye on her. Each time she looked up it seemed he was watching her from some window or other, and she was remarkably pleased. He dared not let her out of his sight. Much more of that alarm business and Georgios and Sofia were going to become very suspicious. Michalis would be the one to get the odd looks then.

Finally she came close to the house and sat on the low balustrade that faced the sea. She was there when he came to the door and spoke to her curtly.

'Lunch will be served in one minute, Miss Stewart.'

'Oh, thank you.' She stood up and smiled brightly and his eyes slid over her very comprehensively, lingering on her slender shape and perfect skin, the shine of her brown hair and the clear grey eyes that looked back at him fearlessly.

'You look about nineteen,' he growled, obviously irritated by that.

'It's the blameless life I've led,' April remarked sweetly, drifting past him like a will-o'-the-wisp and making for the house.

All through lunch his eyes were on her, black, deep and assessing. She began to feel uncomfortable little tingles running down her spine and once or twice when she looked up and met his gaze she felt her cheeks beginning to flush.

'If I take you with me to Athens, will you give me your word that you will not try to escape?' he suddenly

asked. It took her completely by surprise and she just
stared at him in amazement. He looked back seriously
and April could hardly believe it. What did he think she
was—an idiot?

'Certainly not! If I gave my word I'd simply break
it!'

'It is only what I could have expected from you,' he
said tightly.

'What else?' she raged. 'I've never heard such cheek!
I want out of here fast, and if you imagine I'm going
to roam round Athens meekly and then willingly come
back to prison then you can think again!'

Her instant rage obviously amused him because he sat
back and looked at her steadily, his lips quirking, the
dark eyes dancing.

'I have heard that some people become very attached
to their captors.'

'Only in films. This is for real, as you'll find out when
I get away from here.'

'That should take some time if this morning's effort
is an example of your skill. I have observed you prowling
around outside like a caged cat. There is no escape. That
is why I brought you to this particular house. Any more
attempts and you run the risk of injuring yourself. Be
sensible. I can make this a very pleasant time for you if
you will just settle down here. You are amusing and I
like that.'

'I have no intention of settling down to captivity. I'll
keep on trying. If you want me you'll have to catch me.
I have no intention of being amusing.'

'If I wanted you I would catch you,' he said softly,
his eyes narrowed on her suddenly flushed face. She
chose to ignore the innuendo but she felt her heart take
off like a mad thing. She had never thought of any

danger in that direction. She calmed herself and looked haughtily away. He was, of course, goading her. He thought she was some greedy, grasping person who would stop at nothing to get money. He didn't admire a person like that. It made her feel safe again but the seed of doubt had been planted and she was glad when the meal ended and he disappeared once again into his study.

April went towards her room but as she passed the hall the open door of the *sala* drew her attention and something she had not noticed the night before in her agitated state—a telephone. She listened carefully. As far as she could tell, Michalis was busy. The servants were in the kitchen and their next task would be to clear the dining-room. She went quietly into the *sala* and closed the door.

Faced with the phone, she didn't quite know what to do. Should she try the police and risk the language problem? She had no idea how to make a call to England; she would need a code and there was nothing to help her. There were numbers on the phone, though, just like England, and she dialled for the operator, hoping she had not guessed wrongly.

'*Boro na sas voithisso*?'

April stared at the phone in exasperation. Of course they spoke in Greek! What else had she expected?

'Police! Get me the police!' She said it as firmly as she could, praying that the operator also spoke English. If he didn't she was stuck, the telephone quite useless without the international codes.

'*Me sinhorite*?'

April bit her lip with anxiety, glancing back towards the door.

'I don't speak Greek,' she said urgently, raising her voice a little. 'English! Get someone who speaks English.'

There was no reply but the line remained open and she could only hope that somebody else would answer next.

'Can I help you, *despinis*?' It was the most beautiful English she had ever heard and April's shoulders relaxed with relief. Before she could get her mouth open, a strong brown hand took the phone from her and Michalis spoke rapidly into it; he was smiling at something that was said and then he replaced the receiver and turned to her with a look on his face that infuriated her. He looked decidedly smug.

'You are very tiresome, *despinis*,' he pointed out softly. 'Had I not heard the sound of the extension being used you may well have caused trouble. I do not wish to be driven to locking you in your room.'

'One more minute and I would have had the police here,' she said in shaky triumph. 'You may have got rid of them now but they'll be suspicious.'

'I doubt it.' To her annoyance he smiled down at her with a great deal more triumph than she had been able to summon up. 'In the first place they had no idea where the call came from. In the second place, I apologised. I informed them that my niece is staying with me and had been playing a prank. I told them that little girls are sometimes very mischievous. They were amused at your antics.'

'Don't imagine they believed you,' April said scornfully. 'Nobody could mistake me for a little girl.'

'But you never got a chance to converse in English, Miss Stewart. You have a sweet, clear voice. It would be possible to think you were a young girl—providing they could not see you.'

His eyes ran over her suggestively and April stormed out of the room with a very pink face. As she went up the stairs she saw him come from the *sala*, and he was carrying the phone. So that was the end of that! It had nearly worked. She very much doubted if she would get the chance to try it again, but it gave her hope. There would be no need to run to Athens or anywhere else. Once out of here she would use the first phone she came to. All she had to do was escape.

She waited in her room until she heard him in his study and then she waited until she heard him on the phone again. She now knew where it was because he had been standing by the desk when she had come down earlier. The window was there; that was how he had seen her before. When she crept down the stairs she found to her relief that he had partly closed the door. Maybe it had swung almost shut and he had not noticed it?

Whatever the reason it was a good omen, and she slipped outside; this time she skirted the house and came to the woods on the opposite side of the drive, away from the sea. She could not be seen from here; her earlier examination of the surroundings had assured her of that. The wall would stretch around the property with the sea on the one open side and she was not at all particular about which part of the wall she climbed. All she wanted was escape.

This time it was easier. April went well into the woods and then set off briskly for the wall. It was a bit worrying that she had not got away this morning because at some time she would be out there in the dark, and she wasn't at all sure how she felt about that in this alien land. Dora's words about being overpowered came sneakily back into her mind but she pushed them away. She would get to a telephone long before then.

Treacherously her mind observed that she was completely safe at the house, living in luxury. If Michalis hadn't hated her so much he might even be kind. She reminded her disloyal mind that the house was a prison to her and that Michalis Konstantine was a hard and cruel man. He was also starting to worry her with his dark good looks.

He wasn't a bit like Petros. Petros was warm, friendly, cheerful. Michalis was overwhelmingly masculine, sensuous in a very hard sort of way. On the rare occasions he had smiled, his face had taken on a different look, alarmingly attractive. She pulled herself up sharply at this thought. She didn't want to see either of them again. Warm, friendly, cheerful Petros was a liar—unless Michalis was mad, and that wasn't a very soothing conclusion.

April walked along deep in thought, her feet making no sound in the soft pine needles that carpeted the woodland floor. She must be getting close to the wall by now. She looked up and a small scream came tearing into her throat. The shock was so great that she began to shake at once. Michalis was standing there just a little way in front, and after the way she had been thinking about him it was like conjuring up the devil. He was leaning against a tree, his elegant legs crossed one over the other, his arms folded against the hard, powerful chest and the same dark eyes glittered at her like jet.

'How—how did you...? It's not possible!' April looked at him with enormous grey eyes as if he were a magician, and the forbidding frown on his face eased into a wry smile.

'The grounds are escape-proof and entry-proof, *despinis*,' he derided. 'There are cameras all over.' He pointed, and when she looked up there was even one on a tree close by. 'I have been watching your thoughtful progress with great interest.'

'Cameras? Alarms? What have you got in that house—gold bullion?'

'*I* am in the house. Great wealth brings great problems.'

'Somebody might kidnap *you*?' she asked in awe, her mind going into overdrive. It brought a grin to his face, his sudden attraction filling her with yet more awe.

'Only if I am not looking,' he assured her drily. 'You will have observed that I see a great deal.' He eased himself upright and walked towards her with a strange cat-like grace she hadn't noticed before. 'You have been useful in testing the defences. I forgive you. Come, let us go back. You have now tried every escape route and none worked, so give it up.'

'There's the sea,' April reminded him mutinously. It brought a great change from smiling, superior indulgence.

'It is dangerous!' He spun round and stared down at her, his black frown back again, his hands tightly on her shoulders. 'The rocks are slippery and hard—the fall could be fatal. The sea also is not always calm; sometimes there are sudden and unexpected storms. If I imagined you were about to try to get to the beach...'

'Then let me go!' April demanded stubbornly.

'I will not let you go.' He stood staring into her eyes and as far as she could tell he was going to hypnotise her. His eyes seemed to be holding hers with no effort, and they seemed to be blacker, bigger, completely without end. A peculiar light was glowing in their depths and she suddenly found it hard to breathe.

'Stop doing that!' She snatched her eyes away and looked down at her feet, hanging on to the thought of her trainers as if life depended on it.

'Doing what?' There was laughter in his voice and she raised her head indignantly, meeting eyes that were now laughing too.

'You were trying to hypnotise me!'

He gave a great shout of laughter and let her go, turning back towards the house and clearly expecting her to follow. It annoyed her and she stood there without moving.

'Come,' he said softly without turning round. 'If you run I will catch you and take you back to the house over my shoulder. I will then have ceased to be amused at your wild imaginings.'

'Don't think you can force your will on me in any way whatsoever!' April snapped, trailing along behind him. He turned his head and gave her an amused, glittering glance.

'I have not yet tried, Miss Stewart,' he reminded her. 'Do not put it to the test. I have already observed that your daring far outweighs your skill.'

'It's time you also observed that your brother is a liar,' April sniffed crossly. It wiped the smile from his face and he turned back and took her arm impatiently.

'Let us not get into that particular argument again,' he advised. 'It merely reminds me of your character, and as I am stuck with you for some considerable time I would like to forget it. Come along. I have more to do with my time than chase after you.'

April snatched her arm free and walked along with him, fuming inwardly. He seemed to think she had a split personality. Apparently she was guileless when it came to some things and a skilled adventuress when it came to others. If she had been all he thought she was she would have charmed her way out of here by playing up to him. The thought made her blush hotly and when she glanced up he was looking down at her with frowning concentration.

'You do not submit to women's wiles and cry, I note.'

'That's because I've got a good imagination,' she said tartly. 'When tears of rage threaten I remember that before too long you'll be in prison yourself. It brightens the day.'

'You will visit me?' His lips quirked ironically and she glared at him.

'You forget. I'll be in England, blackening your name to the Press. You can be as superior as you like, Mr Konstantine, but finally—you lose!'

'You may call me Michalis,' he conceded arrogantly.

'You may drop dead!' April stormed. The house was in sight and she took off, running towards it furiously, but she just couldn't go fast enough to escape the dark, sardonic laughter that followed her.

He thought he had won. He thought it was now all over and she was trapped. Well, she wasn't! It was too late now. It would soon be dark, but tomorrow was another day and in spite of his alarming lecture she was not afraid to try the cliff and the sand. He couldn't have built his wall across the sand and there wouldn't be cameras there—unless he was expecting pirates!

It would be laughable if somebody did kidnap him, she fumed as she ran up to her room. She could just see him being bundled into a big blanket and dragged away to some dark, dank hut. It seemed that Dora had been right about Greeks. She was trapped by one who was power-crazed, and she had done nothing wrong at all. Petros had lied wickedly and he was free as a bird. But then, Petros was a Konstantine. She was nothing. After kidnapping her and telling her she was nothing that man had the nerve to invite her to call him Michalis! April went to shower and put aside her plans for morning. Tomorrow she would be up with the lark and well away before this odd household stirred itself. And she would show him who had more daring than skill!

This time she managed to be up early. It was only just light as far as she could tell. Now she would be able to get away. She was just about to get out of bed when her door opened and, to her horror, Michalis stood there regarding her suspiciously.

'What do you want?' She slid under the sheets and looked at him over the top, and it did nothing to amuse him.

'I wish to speak to you sensibly.' He came a step into the room and she reached across for her watch. 'You may rest assured that my intentions are completely honourable.'

'Kidnapping is not honourable,' April retorted, 'and it's only six-thirty!'

'I am aware of it. As you are already awake I cannot see the harm in speaking to you. This morning the household is on the move earlier because I have to go into Athens. I had hoped to avoid it but I cannot.'

'Don't mind me.' April tried to hide her glee and managed it as far as she knew. Her words, however, did not set his mind at rest.

'I *do* mind you, Miss Stewart. I am aware that left to your own devices you will get into mischief and probably into danger. In a moment Sofia will bring breakfast to you, but first I have come to ask you once again. Will you give me your word not to try to escape if I take you to Athens with me?'

'No!' She had no desire to go to Athens with him. He would be constantly on guard and she had no idea where he would be going. If he left her here she could escape at leisure.

'Very well.' He walked right into the room and across to the dressing-table. He had her handbag in his hands before she had any idea of what he was about.

'What are you doing? How dare you touch my things?' She shot up in bed and regarded him furiously, but it was already too late. He had her passport in his hand and in a second he also had her return half of the air ticket and her money.

'I am clipping your wings. My trip to Athens is necessary, urgent. I cannot leave you here. You would simply run away, and nothing that Georgios could do would stop you. I therefore intend to take you with me—minus your passport, money and ticket. It will somewhat cramp your style.'

'Give it back at once!' April stormed, but he walked to the door and slanted her a look of impatience.

'When we return. Have your breakfast and then dress for travelling. I will expect to see you downstairs and ready in one hour. I have a meeting this morning and it is a long way.'

His eyes moved over her bare shoulders, her slender arms, and then he closed the door. She was flushed and slightly shaken after that look, but she was also fuming. It was beyond belief! What did he intend to do with her while he had this meeting—take her with him and tie her to a chair? If he had left her behind she could have escaped today with no problems. As it was she would lose another whole day.

Still, Athens was full of people, many of whom would speak English, and there would be an embassy; every place had an embassy surely? Athens most certainly would. And she would be right there, close to the airport without any long trip across country. It might be that this very day she could denounce him for the villain he was. Things were not bad after all. He had played right into her hands. By the time Sofia came with her breakfast she was resting back on the pillows and smiling happily.

CHAPTER FOUR

LATER, dressed in a pale blue suit and white shoes, she went down to the hall and he was just coming from his study. He stopped to watch her walk down the stairs and she felt a stab of anxiety. He was so big and powerful that it seemed madness to pit herself against him. He was in a grey suit with pristine white shirt and a red tie. His handsome face always seemed to shock her now and she couldn't quite understand why. She had glared at him often enough to know how he looked.

It was probably because he did not look like a criminal and was behaving out of character. One thing was sure—he had a towering feeling of his own importance. He must have, to think he could get away with this. He even thought he could take her among people and still get away with it. She looked right at him and he frowned, his eyes coming from their contemplation of her face and hair.

'As you are ready we will leave at once,' he rasped. 'Please remember that you are in high heels. It would be unwise to leap from the car and attempt to run away when the gates are opened.'

'I know I'm trapped for now,' April assured him, sliding into the Mercedes as he held the door for her. 'I've given in for the moment.'

'I doubt it,' he muttered, starting the car and taking it in a long, sweeping turn to face the drive and those impossible gates.

'Am I to attend the meeting with you?' April asked primly as they left the house behind and sped down the drive.

'You are not. I do not think my business associates would appreciate the problem you present. They may be charmed and wish to help.'

'Surely not? If they know you then they must be splendid. I'm nothing, remember?'

'You, Miss Stewart, are big trouble,' he snapped.

'I intend to be.' They went through the gates that opened again as he approached and she still didn't quite see what he touched on the dashboard. They closed again too with that awful finality. 'So if I'm not to go with you, what am I to do?' she asked pleasantly. 'Does that leave me wandering around looking at the sights?'

'It does not. I intend to lock you up.'

'In the car?' April glanced at him scornfully, thinking how she would shout and scream to attract passers-by.

'I have a place,' he murmured, and the thought of the dark, dank hut came back to her mind, scaring her and making her grab for the door. It was securely locked and he shot her a look of extreme exasperation.

'I'm getting out!'

'At this speed? You astonish me, *despinis*. A woman of your talents wishing to injure herself, perhaps end up disfigured? How would you then chase wealth?'

'I just want to go home,' April whispered, very close now to those feminine tears.

'So you shall,' he promised grimly. 'It will, however, be when I decide to let you go and not before. If you had given me your word you could have gone to the shops, enjoyed yourself.'

'Would you have taken my word?'

'I think I would. You are an oddity.'

'I'm not as odd as you,' April sniffed. 'Anyway,' she added thoughtlessly, 'I don't want to go to the shops. It's probably expensive.'

'I would have given you money,' he assured her quietly. 'I realise you have little of your own.'

'I don't want your money or anyone else's money,' April snapped, blushing and feeling full of shame. 'You're quite despicable, aren't you? To be wealthy and—and flaunt it in people's faces is disgraceful.'

'I was attempting to be kind.' He looked at her in exasperation but she glared back.

'No, you weren't! You imagine that money is all I think of.'

'Not according to Petros,' he informed her scathingly. It was his final insult and she subsided into gloomy silence. He had never once doubted his brother. Did she look like a seductress? She blurted it out angrily.

'Do I look like a seductress?'

'No,' he said grimly, his dark eyes on the road. 'You look innocent, even though you are wilful and annoying. However, I cannot take the chance. Petros is to be engaged next week. His future bride will come to the island with her parents and everything will be settled.'

'I almost feel sorry for him,' April said bitterly. 'You're a tyrant.'

'He has known her since he was a child!' Michalis snapped. 'Until you came into his life he desperately wanted to marry her. Now, apparently, he can only think of you.' His eyes slid over her appreciatively. 'I can imagine why, but you are not suitable, not what he needs. He would regret it and a sweet girl's heart would be broken. She would be shamed in front of all her friends and relatives and my own family would be broken up with disputes. I know Petros, but *nothing* will convince

me that you are an innocent victim. He was too im-
passioned when he spoke of you, and I have seen your
escapades. I think you would stop at nothing to get your
own way.'

'Then there's nothing more to be said.'

'Nothing at all.'

The house was in one of the best suburbs of Athens. It
stood at the corner of a street. It was stone-built and
elegant, a shallow flight of steps to the black front door.
On one side was a small park and to the other side houses
of similar build, small town houses that looked expensive. April could imagine Michalis having a hide-
away like this. The whole street was deserted. It was, of
course, sheer chance, but by now she had the decided
feeling that he could just about do anything he wished,
even if it came to wishing people away.

She was not foolish enough to attempt a get-away in
the street and, in any case, his words in the car had quite
subdued her and left her crestfallen. When he opened
the door for her she just got out and walked dejectedly
to the house. There were shutters to every window, each
one tightly closed, giving it an alarming look that further
depressed her. Its silent front looked down on the street
with a sort of severity, and she knew this was where he
intended to leave her, locked up.

Surprisingly it was not either dark or gloomy in the
house. They stepped into a hall with white-painted stairs
leading upwards, but Michalis ignored these. He led her
into a room that was clearly the *sala*. There were white
bookcases reaching the ceiling on some walls, the brightly
tiled floor was strewn with pale rugs and the settee and
chairs were also white. There were pretty touches, from

paintings to plants, and through louvred white doors was a dining-room.

It was light because the shutters were also louvred but very solid-looking nevertheless. She eyed them bitterly.

'How do you know I won't open the shutters and go?' she muttered.

'They are locked, very securely. The shutters throughout the house are locked so save yourself the trouble of exploration.' He went through to a small neat kitchen and began opening doors and looking inside. The fridge brought a quirk of irritation to his mouth. 'There are plenty of things to drink,' he informed her stiffly, 'but no milk. If you want tea there is powdered milk in the cupboard.'

He went up the stairs and she trailed along behind, becoming more interested as she peered into a very feminine bedroom. The bathroom too was well equipped with the sort of things a woman would feel were essential. The shutters here were also locked—at least they were firmly closed, and she assumed they were locked as he had said.

'Can't you at least open the shutters up here?' she asked irritably. 'I'm not likely to jump into the street and kill myself.'

'You would probably try to get down with no thought of danger,' he snapped. 'I do not trust your judgement. In any case, you would certainly attempt to attract passers-by.'

'You've got a fetish about prisons, haven't you?' April asked angrily. 'Suppose I yell my head off? The people next door will hear and investigate.'

'The house next door is unoccupied. This street is a little too expensive for most people.'

'This is a woman's house. This isn't your house. Of course you probably pay the rent.' She looked at him scathingly and he looked coldly back.

'I own the house. But you are quite right. A woman lives here. At the moment she is away.'

'A mistress,' April concluded with further scorn. 'I can see you have one set of rules for yourself and quite a different set for other people. I'm to be locked up because you imagine I'm involved with Petros, but you can set up a woman here and think it quite all right!'

'You would not have been locked up if you had stayed in your own country!' He stared at her furiously. 'I have explained the circumstances. As to myself, I am not about to become engaged and the woman in question is not intent on getting my money. She has plenty of her own.'

'Yes, I can see it would make her above suspicion,' April said bitterly. 'Don't be too complacent. She's probably wanting to collect a bit more.'

'You think a woman would only want me for my money?' he enquired silkily, coming towards her.

'I don't concern myself with your affairs. I just want to go home.' April backed off hastily because she saw a very speculating look in his eyes and she realised they were quite alone. It would perhaps be a good idea to stop goading him and simply get out of here when he left. There must be some way out. It wasn't a dungeon.

'How wise you are,' he said drily. 'It is a good idea to put a little distance between us. Much more of your clever comments and I may be tempted to prove that there is more to me than money.'

April found herself staring into his eyes again, the hypnotised feeling coming back, and she made a great effort and spun around, walking off down the stairs, her cheeks burning. He came down behind her, going no further than the hall.

'I must leave for my meeting.' He glanced at his watch and looked at her impatiently. 'We will not be back at the house for lunchtime, as you can well imagine. It will be necessary to eat. Unless you wish to go hungry we will be obliged to go to a restaurant. Any sign of mutiny there and we will leave without food. It is entirely up to you.' When she didn't answer he glared at her and walked out, locking the door securely behind him, and April went into instant furious action.

If she could open the front door it would be the easiest line of escape. She searched the drawers in the kitchen and came up with a long thin knife. In spite of many attempts, though, she couldn't make any impression on the door. It was irritating, considering that they did it in films all the time. Maybe the locks on the shutters would be easier to handle?

They were not. She tried every one and there was not so much as a creak. She abandoned the knife and went to the bedroom to search for scissors, but they proved to be no use either. This house was tight as a drum and she was right where she had been before—captured.

The feverish activity had made her hot and she longed to throw the windows open and let in some air. She peered through the cracks in the shutters and saw that the street outside now looked hotter than it had been when they had arrived. She had not noticed the heat when she had stepped into here. It had been such a sharp contrast to the sunny street.

She felt stifled, claustrophobic. He didn't care if she collapsed in here. She went from room to room but each place was the same. Under her blue linen suit she wore no blouse and she was even a little timid about opening the jacket in spite of the fact that she was alone. The thought of him suddenly walking in and finding her like that made her feel hotter than ever.

She found a cold drink but it only cooled her for a little while. She got another one out and rolled the can across her forehead but she was hot all over—hot, sleepy and agitated as she had never been in her life. Michalis was beginning to hurt with his scathing attitude and comments. If she didn't get away soon she might just have a good cry and disgrace herself.

She was horrified to discover that she had got used to him, accustomed to seeing his tall, powerful frame, his black hair and dark eyes. She was used to his voice and his odd quirks of humour. Heavens! On several occasions she had even found him protective. She remembered what he had said about people becoming attached to their captors. It wasn't going to happen to her!

She made another frantic attempt to get the front door open and it just about finished her off. At this rate she would be lying unconscious in the hall when he came back. She went up the stairs and back into the bedroom. If his mistress had anything cool to wear she was going to borrow it.

The wardrobe was empty, completely cleaned out. There was nothing at all in the chest of drawers or the dressing-table drawers. She sat on the bed wearily and then closed the door, took off her suit and lay down to rest, her slender figure clad only in brief panties and equally brief bra. She would lie here until she heard him come in and then she would jump up and dress. It was the obvious solution.

April fell asleep. It was something she should have expected but it never occurred to her. She had been battling and making escape attempts since she had arrived in Greece and, resilient though she was, it had been an exhausting time. Now with the addition of the heat of the city and her attacks on the door and shutters she had worn herself out.

When she opened her eyes, alerted by some instinct, Michalis was standing in the doorway, and she was stunned to find him there. It left her momentarily disorientated and then realisation hit her and she grabbed for the loose cover of the bed, frantically trying to cover herself.

'You would stop at nothing to get your own way, would you?' he said softly. 'What is this supposed to be—an attempt to allure me into letting you go, or have you been thinking about diverting your attention to me?'

'I fell asleep.' She hugged the cover closely around her, feeling too embarrassed to really defend herself.

'Or pretended to,' he suggested ironically. 'I can well understand my brother's desperation to see you. I know already that you are desirable, Miss Stewart. There really was no need at all to make the point so obviously.'

April was so filled with shame that she couldn't meet his eyes. She could understand how it looked, and he was not about to give her the benefit of the doubt any more than he had ever done.

'I—I didn't mean to fall asleep,' she whispered, looking away frantically. 'I felt tired and I—I was just lying down.'

'There are comfortable chairs in the *sala*, but of course it would have looked too obvious there, as I can understand. Finding you almost naked in the *sala* would have certainly aroused my suspicions,' he agreed derisively. 'So what am I supposed to do now, *despinis*? Am I to join you on the bed, make love to you, lose my self-control?'

'I was hot!' The tears of shame suddenly escaped, pouring down her face. 'You locked me into this stifling house and left me to suffocate. I—I couldn't bear the heat!'

For a moment he just stared at her, the derision dying from his face. The tears streamed down her face like drops of silver light and he muttered under his breath in his own language, taking a step towards her and then stopping.

'I forgot to turn on the air-conditioning. *Theos*! It never entered my mind.'

He turned and strode out of the room and a few seconds later she heard the sound of the air-conditioning unit flare into action. Cool air began to blow from vents low on the floor but it made very little difference to April. She just sat there and cried. It had all been too much for her. The way he had captured her and isolated her. The scorn he poured on her and now this final humiliation. She cried without sound but she was crying all the same, shaming herself even more. She was wrapped in the cover, her knees drawn up, her head resting on them. She wanted to go home so much that she was ready to scream and scream. Michalis had robbed her of every bit of her spirit and now she was too embarrassed to even answer back.

'Forgive me, *pethi*. I am very cruel to you.' She felt him sit beside her on the bed although she had never heard him come back, and she cringed away. 'Don't do that,' he said softly. 'I'm not going to hurt you. Have I hurt you since I first met you?'

'You've kept me locked up and now you've tried to smother me!' She lifted tear-drenched eyes and found him close, looking down at her. His lips tilted in a wry smile.

'I do not understand "smother",' he confessed in amusement. It was all right for him to be amused. He hadn't been shamed and humiliated.

'It's suffocate, choke, stifle!' April glared at him and he nodded ruefully.

'I did not realise how hot it would be in here. I am accustomed to the heat. I forgot that your English skin would become uncomfortable.' He shrugged. 'In any case, I was too busy arguing with you to remember the air-conditioning.'

He suddenly cupped his hand around her face, tilting it back up when she looked away.

'Are you going to forgive me?'

'You think you can say anything to me,' April sniffed, and he wiped her tears with warm fingers.

'I have attempted several times to be kind to you.'

'You can't seem to understand that I'm a prisoner, can you?' she said fiercely. 'No amount of kindness can wipe that out. No matter what you believed, all you had to do was put me back on the plane. You wouldn't have been forced into pretending kindness because we would never have met again. I don't want to marry Petros and he's lying about us!'

His gentle grip on her face tightened to pain and all the indulgence left his voice.

'I do not wish to speak of Petros! Each time you speak his name it reminds me that you are not the beautiful, bright creature you appear to be. Do not speak of him again. Lies are useless because he did not conjure you up out of his imagination. You are here, beautiful, tempting, and I know that if I relax my attention for one minute you will escape and go to him.'

'I won't!'

'I hope you are speaking the truth,' he said menacingly, 'because if you do escape I will follow you out to the island and settle things in an entirely different way. Like this.'

His hand left her face and slid into her hair, tightening cruelly and tilting her face up to his. She panicked but he held her fast and his mouth caught hers in a hot, fierce kiss that left her breathless. All other kisses faded from her mind and her frantic hands plucked at his sleeves uselessly as her mind swirled.

He forced her lips apart and deepened the kiss until her struggles stopped and she simply made small whimpering sounds that were frightening to her own ears. When he lifted his head to look down at her intently, his eyes on her bruised lips, all she could do was stare at him, mesmerised.

'It would perhaps be easier than constantly guarding you,' he murmured thoughtfully. 'My brother would not want a wife who was already my woman.'

'I—I'd kill you,' April whispered through trembling lips, and his hand captured her face again as he laughed.

'Do not tempt me to prove how easy it would be to bring you enjoyment. You are not immune to me and as you are so experienced it would be a mutual pleasure.'

He let her go and stood, his eyes flashing over her, and she realised that the cover was dislodged and she was once again lying there almost entirely uncovered and shaking with reaction.

'Get dressed,' he ordered, 'and remember what I have said. Do not tempt the fall of fire. You are in Greece. England is far away.'

He went out and April made her shaking legs move. She had never expected anything like that, villain though he was. She was convinced too by his words and actions.

He would not hesitate to do anything he threatened, and after the mind-stopping effect of that kiss she was not at all sure how long she would fight.

When they got to the restaurant she would risk everything and run away. He would never dine in any unpleasant place. It would be smart, exclusive, the people cosmopolitan. They would understand English; after all, *he* did. At the very least they would understand 'Help!'. She couldn't risk waiting any longer. It had to be now. She dressed and went downstairs, outrage overcoming the effect of the kiss.

He was in the kitchen and as she came in he turned and spoke to her as if nothing at all had happened up in the bedroom. He ignored her frosty looks.

'I am making lunch,' he informed her pleasantly. 'I stopped to buy bread and cheese, olives and fruit. I also bought milk for you. There are some very nice biscuits with honey and almond. We will eat here and then we will go back home.'

April just stared at him, wondering if he could read her mind. Another escape plan dashed!

'It's not home,' she said stiffly. He might have dismissed what had happened between them but she could not. 'Why are we eating here?'

'Perhaps I want to be alone with you?' he suggested drily, walking through to the dining-room with some of the lunch and coming back to get more. 'On the other hand, perhaps I too have a good imagination. I can imagine, for example, how embarrassing it would be if you should decide to stand up in a crowded restaurant and scream at the top of your voice. They would be astonished and suspicious. I might even be detained long enough for you to make good your escape.'

'What makes you think they wouldn't slap you into gaol for a good long while?' April asked heatedly, furious that her desperate plan was thwarted.

'I am a little too well-known, a little too wealthy and a little too powerful,' he assured her smoothly. 'They may, however, try to take you away from me and put you into a place where you could be observed and classified. I really would not like that.'

She knew perfectly well what he meant, and it was quite likely with her luck lately. She could imagine that he would go scot-free while she was sent to a hospital for the mentally unstable.

'Come along,' he invited, his lips quirking with amusement at her expression. 'Everything is ready. I have even made tea for you.'

'I expect it's dreadful,' she said churlishly.

'It is not. I know how to make tea. I went to university in England. I frequently made it on the little gas stove in my room.' He was grinning at her, looking dangerously charming, and she glared at him. Little gas stove! He had probably been sent to one of the best colleges in Cambridge or Oxford. His father would have bought him a suite of rooms with a cringing servant.

'Have you got a father?' she enquired waspishly, sitting down and pouring her tea with a very bad grace. His black brows rose in astonishment.

'I *did* have one, a long time ago. I did not suddenly appear one dark night, fully formed and raging. You sometimes ask strange questions, *pethi*.'

'Don't call me that!' April snapped. 'I don't know what it is but it sounds patronising.'

'It is an endearment.'

'I am not endeared to you so I can do without it, thank you. Your father must have been very lax with you.

Obviously you feel too self-important, power-crazed. It should have been smacked out of you as a child.'

He stopped with his cup halfway to his lips.

'Are you goading me into making love to you, April?' he enquired softly. 'All you have to do is ask. I have told you it would solve a lot of problems. I would even take you out to the island and let you meet everyone. It would only be necessary to announce that you are my woman and things would be quite settled!'

April blushed painfully and stopped talking, her defiance wiped away. When she tried to lift her cup, her hands were trembling so much that she had to put it down again, and she stared at the food on her plate woefully.

'Eat,' the dark voice ordered softly. 'You are perfectly safe. I only make love to the willing. The danger lies not in my amorous intentions but in your frequent and misguided attempts to escape. So far you have not injured yourself because I have watched over you. Perhaps one day I will not be looking.'

'There was only the gate,' April muttered, refusing to look up. 'If you hadn't caught me the second time I would have climbed the wall and got away.'

'You would not,' he informed her seriously. 'You would have met with the same noise and this time you would have fallen. The wall has no convenient handholds. The alarm system covers the whole estate.'

'Why do you lock yourself up?' She looked up at him in astonishment and he sat back, regarding her darkly.

'I have told you. Great wealth can bring great danger. I do not lock myself up unless the place is isolated. I am not locked up here.'

April pursed her lips and looked pointedly at the closed shutters, and he got up at once and opened two of them.

'Aren't you scared I'll dash to the window and scream?' she asked sarcastically, a little of her embarrassment having faded and some of her normal spirit surfacing.

'I would kiss you into silence,' he informed her evenly, sitting down and getting on with his meal. 'Now that you know all about me, eat your lunch. I would like to be home long before dark. I have things to do.'

This time she didn't tell him that it was not home; she kept silent and ate. Things were now worryingly different because he had come up with a sure way to stop any attempt at escape. Her mind wandered back to the house and lingered on the cliff, the wide expanse of sea and that strip of beach. She wondered rather hysterically if it was mined.

It was her only avenue of escape now, and she would have to try it. If she had ever been tempted to just sit this out and wait for him to let her go, the thought was now crushed permanently. She could still feel those fierce lips on hers and the feeling made her skin hot. Escape was essential. Tomorrow, tomorrow. It had to be soon. Danger grew with each day. Somehow she was becoming too involved with this man.

Next morning April awoke to a grey-looking sky. It didn't look much like an escape day. She had her breakfast and still lingered in bed, suddenly lacking the energy to spring up and make a dash for the cliff. The drive back from Athens had not been filled with embarrassed silence as she had expected. Michalis had talked to her as if they were old acquaintances.

He had talked about his country, about the ancient Greece and its treasures, about the old Pilgrim's Road that led from Athens, part of it still there to this day.

'Anyone could take the road,' he said. 'There were no racial restrictions. The one rule was that anyone going to the end, to the temple, must speak Greek. And they must not reveal what wonders awaited them.'

'What do you think happened?' April asked, intrigued.

'Probably something very trivial to the modern mind,' he laughed. 'Most mysteries are very simple when dragged out into the open.'

She sat in comfort and listened to the dark, deep voice, and after a while he glanced across at her.

'April. Promise me that you will not try to escape again,' he asked quietly.

'I—I can't.' Instantly she sat up straight in her seat, her nerves jangling. He made no comment but the friendly talking stopped and they were right back where they had started, heading for the house, captor and victim, angry silence between them.

Things had not improved at dinner and when the telephone rang he took it in the dining-room where there was another extension. She could not understand any of the conversation but he was quite cold and angry. Apparently somebody was attempting to argue with him, some misguided person, because he suddenly snapped out words like ice and put the phone down.

She was not about to enquire, it being none of her business, but he told her anyway and she found out that it was very much her business.

'That was your lover,' he rasped. 'He was enquiring about you. As I had volunteered to collect you he wondered why you had not appeared on the island. Do you not think that a little tardy, Miss Stewart? One would have expected a lover to be more impatient, to worry about his beloved. I told him you had not arrived.'

'Didn't you expect him to enquire?'

'I expected him to enquire on the first night,' he snapped. 'My anger was for an entirely different reason. He threatened to go to England and get you.'

April looked up in astonishment.

'But—but I'm only a friend and even that was now some time away.'

'Only a friend? You expect me to believe that? Do not fear, *despinis*. He will not go to England. I have forbidden it.'

'Then maybe he'll defy you!' April seethed, angry herself at this constant battering of her self-esteem.

'My family do not defy me,' he grated. 'This is Greece and I am the head of the Konstantine family. Defiance does not happen, nor do unsuitable marriages—if that is what he has in mind. You should not hope too much, though. It is probably his idea of a last fling.'

April got up and walked out of the dining-room without looking back. He would never change his mind. She was a scarlet woman, an adventuress, utterly unsuitable to be anything but a guarded prisoner. At the moment England seemed very far away.

Now in the unexpectedly grey light of the morning she realised she was no longer defiant. She was simply miserable, and she was going to be more miserable with each day that passed. When she went down after breakfast he was waiting for her, his looks threatening.

'This afternoon,' he said icily, 'I am going out. It will just be for a little while but once again it is necessary. Do not forget that the wall is dangerous. Stay close to the house. There may be a storm.'

April didn't answer because there was nothing to say, and after one grim look at her he went to his study. She knew he was angry at being trapped here himself, and no doubt his business empire would crumble if he was away for long. It was useless to plead with him. She knew she would have to go when he went out. He might not go out again.

She stayed in her room watching the sea and planning. This time she would have to take a sweater. The wind was getting up and the tree-tops were tossing more each minute. The climb to the beach was a risk, but it had to be taken. She would put her sweater on and just take her bag. Luckily Michalis had been true to his word and given back her passport, money and ticket last night.

Any softening on his part had quite gone after Petros had phoned, and he had looked at her suspiciously as he'd handed them over. She had them now, though, and that was all that mattered. Today she must escape because he was not about to simply let her go.

He went immediately after lunch and she didn't even give him time to get to the gate. Georgios and Sofia were in the kitchen, dealing with the lunchtime dishes, and as the Mercedes pulled away April raced to her room, gathered her handbag, put on her sweater and ran downstairs and out into the wind, making for the cliff with all speed.

She dared not even glance at the sea. She knew exactly how it would look, and there was no alternative but to go. She lowered herself over the edge, feeling for footholds, and then began to move downwards, her hands clinging to the soft turf at the top of the cliff. Slowly but surely. It was not far to the beach and it was better to be wet than stay here.

The storm hit with astonishing ferocity before she had even moved from the top. Without warning the rain came and it came in a deluge. Within seconds the sky was black as night, lightning forking across it in the distance, and she was soaked to the skin instantly.

Her foot that had been feeling for the next hold on the rocks slipped on a surface that was now wet and dangerous, and she knew that if she moved at all the rock she stood on would also become impossibly slippery. The grass she clung to was softer, feeling as if it would come away in her hands.

Foolishly she looked down then. The sea was boiling up on to the rocks, their sharp, jagged edges like dragon's teeth waiting to devour her. She was trapped with no hope of moving because any movement might send her hurtling down. Michalis was out, and this time he could not come to save her. Georgios and Sofia thought she was in her room and they would not intrude.

Nobody in the whole world knew where she was—only Michalis and his servants knew she was alive even. She hung on to the grass, not daring to move either her feet or her hands. This time she had taken on more than she could cope with.

CHAPTER FIVE

THE car came tearing up the drive, wet, black and shiny in the lights from the house. April began to scream his name before the car had even stopped, but he did not hear her. The wind was so loud, the rain violent, and she saw him get out of the car in a hurry. He must have taken off his jacket as he had left because he was in shirtsleeves, and he was instantly wet as he stepped out of the car and made for the house.

She would never be able to hang on until he discovered she had gone again. She screamed his name louder, desperately.

'Michalis! Michalis!'

He spun round, peering into the gloom, and when she shouted again he saw her. April could feel her foot slipping as he raced towards her, and she was terrified. She could hear the sea raging below, and her hair was plastered to her head, strands of it across her face. Her hands were now cold and gripping was more difficult by the second.

He flung himself down on the cliff-top, grabbing her by the upper arms, his dark face close to hers.

'Michalis! Michalis!' She couldn't seem to stop whimpering his name, and he hushed her urgently.

'I've got you; keep very still. Do not relax. Now, carefully, one hand at a time, let go of the grass and grip my arms.'

'I—I'll pull you over!' The rain was pouring down on them and she was too frightened to move. She seemed to be locked into the position with no hope of ever moving.

'Do as I say. Keep your feet on the rocks and grip my arms.'

It took all her courage to let the grass go, but she obeyed. His hands tightened and then slid beneath her arms, gripping her so strongly that she gasped with pain.

'Put your arms around my neck and hang on,' he ordered, and when she did he began to lift her, easing her up over the edge and on to the soaking grass at the top. She collapsed beside him but he had no intention of leaving her there for even a second. He stood and looked down at her and then pulled her to her feet. Now he was not calm and rational; his eyes were blazing and he looked almost murderous.

'You little fool!' He grasped her shoulders and pulled her against him. 'Seconds and you would have been dead!'

April was too shocked to speak. They stood there facing each other, rain drenching them. It was running off their faces, off their hair. His shirt was clinging to him, wet, muddy and grass-stained, but neither of them thought of discomfort. She was shaking and weak. Michalis was blackly angry.

He cupped her wet face in hard hands and glared at her, and all she could do was look back helplessly.

'If I had not been suspicious,' he raged, his chest heaving with anger. 'If I had not come back...'

He choked on the words and then pulled her face to his, capturing her mouth in wild anger, crushing her lips and tightening his hands around her face. April was crying but he did not know. Her tears mingled with the rain, moved from her face to his as they stood locked together like enemies. She was numb with reaction. She never even noticed when his hand moved from her face and cupped her wet hair as his arm came around her.

'You would have been on those rocks,' he muttered, his face against hers, 'broken, lifeless, swept into the sea.'

'Oh, please don't!' April was shaking in his arms, frightened, shocked and unable to even think.

He looked down at her in the pouring rain and he could see then that her eyes were filled with tears. The dark eyes looked into hers and he began to kiss her again, slowly and deeply. It eased the shock, warmed her, and the trembling stopped as the kiss went on endlessly. He drew her closer and closer until their wet bodies were almost bound together, and it was only as he at last raised his head that April realised she had wound her arms around his neck, that she was clinging on to him as tightly as he was holding her. She felt safe with his arms around her. His power seemed to protect her from everything.

'Come into the house,' he said abruptly, releasing her as if he had just come to his senses. He moved away and April staggered, gasping as pain suddenly seared through her ankle.

'I—I've twisted my foot.'

'If that is all that has happened to you then you have got off very lightly,' he grated, back to anger. It wasn't all that had happened to her. He had held her, kissed her, rescued her yet again. The shaking wasn't just fear. For a few seconds she had felt almost part of him, and it had delighted her. Now it frightened her.

'I'm sorry.' She hung her head and limped forward, but he scooped her up into his arms and made for the house. The wind was now wilder, lashing the rain at them, and April was back to shivering. He looked down at her in the lights of the house and then simply started up the stairs, carrying her easily. Georgios and Sofia had not appeared, and probably they did not know that anyone had come into the house. She was grateful for that.

'You need a hot shower,' he muttered crossly. 'So do I. When you are ready I will look at that ankle.'

He put her down in her room, close to the bathroom, and turned away as if he was just going to walk off, and she wanted to plead with him, to tell him she would never try such tricks again. She wanted to reassure herself as much as she wanted to reassure him.

'Michael.' Her soft voice brought instant fury and he spun to face her.

'Do not confuse me with my brother!' he snapped. 'I am Greek. My name is Michalis. Speak to Petros as you wish but when you speak to me remember who I am!'

He walked out and slammed the door and April limped to the bathroom; then she stood shivering under the hot, stinging spray of the shower. There was still panic inside her. She would not forget the fear for a long time. In her mind she could see the cruel rocks, the equally cruel sea, and she stood there helplessly as the water poured over her.

If he had not come back she would now be dead. He had told her that and it was true. She knew she would never again try to escape. It had occupied almost all her thoughts since she had been here, but now it was crushed completely.

She put on her dressing-gown and sat on the bed to rub her hair dry. How would he treat her now? He would probably send her home. In a way they had both lost because she had at last admitted that she could not get away, and she was too big a liability to be kept here. Perhaps tomorrow he would take her to Athens and put her on a plane. He must know now that she would not dare to get in touch with Petros even if she had wished to.

Any mention of his brother seemed to drive him to rage and she vowed to keep quiet from now on until he let her go. She wished she had simply submitted to captivity from the first. It would have been safer all round.

He came in while she was sitting there, her hair now almost dry, falling to her shoulders in tangled brown waves. Her shivering had stopped although she was still feeling the aftermath of great fear.

'Drink this.' He handed her a glass of brandy, watching her until she began to sip it obediently. 'Let me see that foot.'

The old April would have refused, but she held up her foot, wincing as his fingers probed it gently. He knelt down and she noticed then that he had a bandage and a small pot of something in his hand. She never asked anything. If it was some horrid concoction she was just going to sit here and say nothing at all. Her days of being a nuisance were over. At this moment, every bit of defiance had gone.

'I have borrowed this from Sofia. She is from one of the islands and quite accustomed to dealing with any minor accident. It will be better by morning, or so she informs me.'

'Did she want to know...?'

'She did not. I go my own way and I am not in the habit of explaining myself. They have been with my family for many years. They know me.'

She wasn't surprised. It was hard to imagine anyone questioning him. He had changed into casual trousers and a close-fitting sweater and April looked down at his dark head as he completed his task, skilfully bandaging her ankle and methodically screwing the top on to the jar. She wanted to talk to him but she had a good deal more sense than that.

He walked into her bathroom to wash his hands and she somehow expected it. She wished he would walk out drying his hands and chatting to her. She wanted to smile at him and see that flashing white smile light up his face. It came rarely, but it altered him and it would settle her nerves.

He just walked out and turned to the door.

'If you wish, you may have your dinner served here in your room. It will be easier on the ankle and give you more time to recover from shock. I think it would also be a good idea if you were to get into bed.' She looked away from his still face and nodded, lifting her head swiftly as she heard him move to the door again.

'Please don't just go,' she begged anxiously. 'I—I haven't thanked you for saving me and—and I wanted to tell you that I'll never try to escape again.'

He looked across into her pleading eyes and his usual sardonic looks were entirely gone. He was still and sombre.

'This time I believe you because tomorrow I am putting you on a plane for England. I will have to risk any contact with Petros. There is a limit to how many times I can be around to rescue you. I have developed an instinct about you, but one day it may let me down. Tomorrow you go home.'

April just hung her head, not able to meet the dark, penetrating eyes, and he stood looking at her for a few seconds more.

'You do not want to go, *despinis*? You have become attached to your captor?'

He walked out and April bit her lip in anxiety. She had better not get attached to him. She told herself desperately that tomorrow and the plane home could not come soon enough.

When Sofia brought her dinner, April did not much feel like eating, but she tried. She was too miserable to really enjoy anything. Tomorrow she would leave Greece and never come back. She tried to cheer up. At the moment her spirits were low but she was still suffering from what could have been a very nasty or even fatal episode. She would forget all about Michalis Konstantine. Other men had kissed her. It was just that she had been closed up with Michalis in this house and he had such a powerful personality that he had invaded her thoughts.

He invaded her thoughts every time she tried to relax. And it was useless to tell herself that other men had kissed her. They had not kissed her like that. She would have been furious. She could not have responded like that either. He was too deeply in her mind to be easily dismissed. It was like stepping into a dream and then waking up to find it was gone.

He came when it was very late. He knocked softly on her door and came in when she called. She was just coming from the bathroom and had imagined it was Sofia. She had not expected to see Michalis, and she stood there rather anxiously, her hands clutching her dressing-gown close as he came in and stood in the doorway looking at her.

'I thought you may be asleep,' he said.

'No. I—I don't seem to be tired.'

'It is probably shock. Would you like me to get you something? Another brandy?'

'No, thank you.' April looked away but he did not leave.

'How does your ankle feel?' It felt fine. She moved it experimentally and told him so.

'I think it's all right. It was probably nothing at all.'

'It was slightly swollen. The ointment is supposed to be almost magical, according to Sofia. Well, if you are fine then I will let you go to sleep.'

April couldn't think of anything to say. She wanted to say she was sorry. She wanted to thank him, to make things right somehow, but words would not come. All she could do was stand there looking at him, mesmerised by his power. She knew his face so well, as if she had known him for years instead of days, and his great crime in kidnapping her seemed to have faded to the very back of her mind.

He looked back at her, holding her eyes, his lips tightening at her expression. She looked bewildered, vulnerable and anxious, very different from the girl he had met at the airport, but with the same innocent eyes, so clear and grey, watching him so desperately.

His jaw tightened and his dark eyes narrowed.

'It is not a good idea to gaze at me like that,' he said harshly. 'I still have the taste of you in my mouth and I am a perfectly normal man with normal desires.'

April flushed rose-pink, tearing her eyes away and looking frantically at her clenched hands. She could still taste him too. She could still remember the scent of his skin, the peculiar silken rasp of his face against hers in the pouring rain, the way he had held her so close that they had seemed to be moulded together.

'*Theos*! Speak to me!' he bit out harshly. 'After tomorrow I will never see you again.'

'It—it's what you want,' April managed shakily. His words had brought heated feeling into the room, an intensity that was almost aggressive. 'I'm sorry I ever came and I can promise you that I'll never try to get in touch with——'

'Do not speak his name!' Michalis was beside her before she could finish the sentence, his hands tightly on her arms. 'You remind me. I do not wish to be reminded about what you were to my brother!'

'Why don't you believe me?' She looked up at him mournfully and his eyes moved over her face slowly as if he were touching her.

'Because you are too desirable to be real,' he said bitterly, 'too young, too beautiful to be what you seem. But more than that you came to Greece to a man who has declared his infatuation with you and has given good reasons. You came with a ticket and little else. You were escaping a life you did not want and you were expecting to stay permanently.'

'If that's what you believe then believe it,' April whispered. 'What does it matter after all?'

'Perhaps it matters to me,' he muttered fiercely.

'Why should it? You've made your mind up. It was made up before you ever saw me. You believed Petros. Go on believing him.'

'I do believe him! It matters to me, though, and I wish it did not. I want you myself.'

She just looked up at him, looked into eyes that seemed to be burning with black flames. They caught her, held her, and she trembled, her face paling with the unexpected words. He meant it. She had no doubt about that. His face was taut, a muscle at the side of his mouth pulsing with the effort it took to control his feelings. His hands were moving on her arms, the harsh grip relaxed as he brushed her arms with open palms, his fingers flexing urgently.

April made a small sobbing sound, partly distress and partly excitement, and he let his control snap. Deliberately, slowly, he pulled her to him, wrapping his arms around her and searching fiercely for her mouth. There was no way that she could resist, even though she knew his opinion of her. She was enclosed in arms like iron, her head pushed ruthlessly to his shoulder as he kissed her almost frenziedly.

'You were made for holding, made for desire,' he muttered thickly against her lips. 'Light as a feather, soft as silk with eyes like stars. I want you myself. I want you now!'

He forced her lips apart and she moaned at the invasion of his tongue, sensuous and suggestive, exploring the warmth of her mouth almost secretly. It ran around her parted lips and then plunged back to search for her tongue and caress it roughly. Her hands gripped his waist and then encircled it tightly as flames shot through her, making her legs weak, and she sagged against him to be caught up and brought closer.

Michalis ran his hand down her back, his fingers searching her spine, a low growl of impatience in his throat at the thickness of her robe. He dispatched it easily, dropping it to the floor and bringing her close again. His lips never left hers and she could hear her own laboured breath mingling with his. It was mad, wicked but she was caught up in the fire, wanting to be burned, kissing him back with the same wild urgency.

When his fingers searched her spine again through the thin satin of her nightie she cried out in shock, fierce feeling rippling through her from the very centre of her being. She arched against him and he accepted her soft body eagerly, forcing her to face the reality of his hard desire. It merely drove her further into the abyss. The whole world was a void with only the fire that Michalis offered to cling to, the hard, powerful body a chasm to lead her down into velvet darkness.

'Give yourself to me, *pethi*,' he murmured huskily. His breathing was laboured, uneven, and April could not speak at all. She was overwhelmed, lost in heated darkness, falling faster and faster. All she could do was moan his name as she trembled in his arms and he swung her up to hold her against his chest and walk with her to the bed.

She had no time to recover, to come to whatever senses she had. He put her down gently and came to her at once, gathering her tightly to him.

'You are so beautiful,' he whispered thickly, 'so slender and warm. I want your silken skin against mine, April, your shining hair against my lips.'

He pulled his sweater over his head and threw it to the ground, holding her close as he eased away the thin straps that held her nightie. She was naked to the waist and his face was tight with desire when he looked down at her, his eyes on the rose-tipped beauty of her small, perfect breasts. He touched them gently and she was so sensitised to him that she cried out as feelings shot through her. Her breasts hardened, rising to meet his hands, the nipples sharp and pointed, and his breath hissed through clenched white teeth as he bent over her.

His hands cupped their fullness as his mouth crushed hers but he could not wait to explore her and his teeth tightened gently on her breast, nipping until she cried out with pain and delight, soothing as he took the sharp point into his mouth. He nuzzled against her until she was sobbing in his arms and then he lifted her, sliding away the last of her covering, looking down at the slender beauty he had discovered.

'Only if you are willing,' he breathed harshly, his eyes moodily on her body.

April was so filled with desire she had never felt before that she was almost panicking, frantic for something she had never had, never thought of.

'Yes!' She gasped out the word and he smiled down at her with burning dark eyes. His clothes seemed simply to disappear, because she never noticed him undress. She was too fascinated by the hard, powerful chest, the crisp black hair that feathered across it. She wanted to pull him closer and her hands reached out for him, running over the covering of hair and then tugging impatiently, her fingers curled in the crisp darkness.

He laughed softly and came back to her, moving over her and pressing her into the softness of the bed.

'Soon, *pethi*,' he promised thickly. 'But it will not be gentle and it will not be quick. My desire for you is fierce, savage and bitter. You can surely understand that?'

It brought April back to the room, back to her wandering senses, his warning of ferocity, savagery and bitterness making her realise how powerful was the body that covered her own, how sleek and strong and how determined. His hand slid between them, seeking the source of her desire, and she stiffened, panic-stricken. He thought she was experienced. He believed everything he had heard from Petros. His lips were on her breast and as she stiffened he looked up at her in surprise, his dark eyes meeting hers that were wide, grey and terrified.

'What is it? You are frightened?' he asked.

For a second she could not speak, and his astonishment was turning to anger when she found her voice.

'I—I can't! I've never...'

'Do not play games with me!' He looked down at her, his face taut with passion and rising anger. 'You went up in flames in my arms.'

'I couldn't help it,' April whispered, her eyes filled with terror. 'When you touch me I can't resist but I've never been with anyone. I—I'm frightened.'

For a long minute he looked at her, searching her mind, his hands still flexing on her skin, and then he moved away, tossing her nightie over her and dressing as she lay trembling with her eyes closed.

'You can open your eyes,' he said sharply, and when she did he was standing by the bed, looking down at her. His breathing was still laboured and his eyes still ran over her with open desire but the frenzy was under control.

'I'm sorry,' she whispered, and his face darkened, his eyes narrowed.

'If I thought for one minute that you were playing some dangerous game of reprisal you would be very sorry,' he assured her softly. His gaze moved over her mournful face, her flushed cheeks and wide, clear eyes. 'However, I am not sure.'

He found her dressing-gown and dropped it on the bed beside her.

'Let us hope that your ankle is better by morning, April,' he said quietly, 'because you will be walking on it.'

'To the airport,' she agreed, her face confused and anxious.

'To the island! I intend to get to the bottom of this and you will not see England until I do.'

'You're taking me to the island?' Astonishment stopped her worried looks. 'But Petros is there and— and your family.'

'Yes,' he agreed, his eyes like ice at the sound of his brother's name. 'Petros is there and one of you will tell the truth. I cannot wait to sail there. I will fly you there. I want to see this meeting very much indeed and I want to see it as soon as possible.'

He walked out and closed the door and April began to put on her nightie. If sleep had been far from her before it was even further now. She was still throbbing with feeling, still burning up inside. Her fear had not banished that. The desire was there and it was real. His desire had been real too, fierce and possessive. Now she had to face his family, face Petros and call him a liar in his own home with Michalis standing there like a dark eagle, watching.

How had this happened? How had she been drawn into the dark, burning fire? In these few days she seemed to have lived a lifetime, the power of Michalis surrounding her as if she had no other existence. Even with her eyes closed she could see him, and she wilfully kept him there, in her head, clinging to him as she had clung to him earlier. When he touched her, everything inside her melted and she wanted it to go on and on until the flames burned her, because it was a feeling she had never known before.

April sat beside him next morning in the helicopter. It had taken very little time. She had brought all her things with her and she knew that after this she would be taken to her plane, her connection with the Konstantines severed completely. She was an outsider, ordinary, not suitable to mix with this wealthy clan, nothing.

The weather had cleared overnight and even before she was dressed April heard the sound of a helicopter overhead. As she stood by the window to watch, it had put down slowly on the cliff-top and she could see the pilot, sitting inside, waiting for further orders. Michalis had meant every word he had said. She was going to the island to meet the Konstantine family.

They had flown over several islands and as each one had come in sight she had tensed up inside, preparing herself for the forthcoming ordeal. Each time she had been mistaken, her tension only partly fading as another island came into view, lying beneath them in a blue sea. Anxiety mounted because she did not know how she would face this. Once, Petros had seemed so nice, so ordinary, but now he was someone she did not know at all. They were all strangers except the man who sat silently at her side, his face still and controlled.

Michalis, who had kidnapped her, forcibly kept her isolated, was now the only one she could turn to, and he was not on her side. He was putting his family in order, sorting out his brother's involvement with someone who was an alien, unsuitable intruder into the elevated lives of a wealthy Greek family.

He suddenly shot a lightning glance at her tense face and then touched her arm.

'We are here.' He pointed downwards and April looked worriedly in the direction he indicated. It was an island typical of the ones she had seen already, but much smaller. The helicopter was fairly low and it was not possible to estimate the size, but she could see nothing but green-clad hills rising to mountains. She could see wide beaches between rocky outcrops where the sea lapped with white-topped waves. It looked deserted, like some strange tropical island miles from civilisation, but as they rose to fly over the cliffs that towered below April saw the house.

It was a mansion built with the golden stone of the island. It looked old and dignified and slightly forbidding. They circled above and she saw a swimming-pool, vast gardens all blooming brilliantly, tall trees that must have been imported many, many years ago. The gardens sloped downwards, terraced towards a beach, and as the helicopter turned she had a front-on view of the house.

It spoke of wealth, security and a grandeur she had never seen before.

'The Konstantine fortress,' Michalis murmured. 'My family have owned this place for generations.'

'What about the villages?' April asked, stunned by the look of the place and remembering how Petros had described the village houses, the church, the men who worked on the island.

'There are no villages. There is the house, the mountains, the sea, nothing more.'

'Petros told me there were houses, village people, a church,' she said desperately.

'He was probably trying to assure you that there was safety. He can correct his story in a very few minutes.'

'Maybe he's not there.' April clung to the hope to ease the strain, but his lips tightened angrily.

'Comforting thoughts are of little use,' he rasped. 'He is there, and I will be there also when you face each other. It will be obvious which one of you is lying.'

He did not need to make any threats. It was in his voice. The one found to be lying would wish he or she had never been born. If it was Petros he had made a fool and a villain of his own brother. If it was April she had cheated him last night, tricked him into letting her go after leading him to raging passion. Whatever happened, this was not going to be a happy family reunion and she was going to be an embarrassed and scorned onlooker.

CHAPTER SIX

THEY landed on the great lawn in front of the house. The helicopter was set down like a butterfly, but April hardly noticed. Her eyes were drawn to the house, to the steps and long, deep patio. Moments ago the place had looked deserted but now there were people, servants in the background, eager to watch the landing, and at the front, waiting to greet them, three people she dreaded to meet.

There was Petros of course, in spite of her prayers to the contrary. The other two were women—a dark, pretty girl and a tall, slim woman who even from here April could see was sophisticated, fashionably dressed and wealthy—Madame Konstantine!

How this proud woman would take to the events that were about to unfold, April dared not think. What she did know was that whatever happened *she* was going to be embarrassed and unhappy. Her eyes turned anxiously to Michalis, and he was watching her in that intense, speculating way that she had become used to.

'Your mother . . . !'

'My mother is not to be distressed,' he bit out. 'The meeting between you and Petros will take place when she is not there.'

'But she's there now, and so is he!'

'What a pity both of you did not think of this when you arranged to be together in her house. You will leave it to me. Anything I say you will follow; otherwise I can promise you a good deal of embarrassment and grief.'

'You could have saved any of it by taking me to the plane!'

'I want the truth, all of it!' he rasped, pinning her with cold black eyes. 'I will have the truth this day and I will arrange it in my own way.'

'You act as if you're the one with a grievance. I can assure you that you're both going to be sorry—you *and* Petros!' April snapped, her temper overcoming every other feeling. 'Does your mother know she has two insane sons with criminal inclinations? And what's to stop me storming out there and tackling Petros head-on?'

'I would probably strangle you,' he murmured, climbing down and lifting her to the ground when she would have liked to kick out at him. He might be able to turn her to flames but he was the most arrogant, the most insufferable man. 'Curb that temper. The pilot does not speak English but my family most assuredly do. We are accustomed to civilised behaviour.'

'And what's civilised about you?' April hissed. 'You kidnapped me, forced me into making dangerous escape bids, kissed me...'

'Made love to you,' he added, glancing up at her ironically and making her blush. He spoke to the pilot in his own language, and her luggage was placed on the lawn as the helicopter prepared to leave. 'Let your mind dwell on that last statement,' he advised, turning back to her. 'Open your mouth about anything controversial and I will kiss you into silence in front of everyone. It will set my mother's mind at ease. She will now be utterly bewildered and anxious, wondering which one of her two sons owns this delightful foreigner.'

'Neither of you!' April burst out.

'That is what I wish to find out,' he said threateningly. 'However, I do not wish to find out in front of my mother; therefore do as I have told you. I will do the talking and you will look shy and defenceless. It will touch her heart.'

'You're as bad as Petros!' April told him. The servants had now found an excuse to come forward and at least three of them were intent on her luggage. The Konstantine family were also coming and April wondered what they had thought about this delay while she and Michalis battled.

'I am much worse than Petros, much more dangerous,' he warned her softly. 'However, I am not a liar. I will soon know whether there is one liar or two on this island. I am already aware that there is most certainly one.'

There was no time for more talk and April wished belatedly that she had used the time to plead instead of fight. She could also have done with a little coaching. He had told her to do as he said, but what would he say and would she be quick enough to follow his lead?

There was also the matter of Petros, and she realised that all this meant that Petros had been defiant to Michalis only in the matter of his future wedding. Madame Konstantine knew nothing; neither did his sister. It also meant that Petros could not greet her as anything but an acquaintance. It would be interesting to see how he handled that! At this moment she felt like rushing across to him and doing the strangling herself.

What had he expected but this? If Michalis had not been the man he was, if he had tamely greeted her in Athens and brought her straight here, what would Petros have done then? If he had a plan he had better get it out and look at it because trouble was striding towards him with a black frown on his face.

Petros didn't look at all embarrassed, and it gave April a very nasty shock. The sunny, pleasant face was all smiles and he was coming to meet them as if he had been happily waiting. He had a plan all right, and she knew who was going to suffer for it.

He reached them before his mother and sister, but they were close, and he smiled into her eyes.

'April! You're here at last!' He took her hands and kissed both of them, and her eyes slid anxiously to the rest of the family. They looked perfectly happy about this. She almost panicked. Michalis had his back to her. He was bending to kiss his mother and sister on their cheeks; when he turned round he would no doubt look at her with scorn and make his decision.

'We've heard so much about you, Miss Stewart, and your family's kindness to Petros when he was in England. We expected you last week but never mind; you are here in good time for the celebrations.'

Madame Konstantine came forward regally, a perfectly genuine smile on her face, and April could not prevent her eyes from moving rather desperately to Michalis. Petros had been telling even more lies. He had never met her family. In any case, she had only had her mother when he was there.

'I hope Petros did not forget to tell you that I know April too, *Mitera*. If I had not known her she would not have been able to find him and take him under her wing. No doubt he would have been in every kind of trouble during his college days without her assistance.' Michalis gave her one of his wonderful smiles and April tried not to look stunned. What was this supposed to mean? Had these two impossible males been in touch and concocted this tale or was Michalis playing it by ear, warning his brother as he was also warning her?

'No, he did not tell us that, but he does not like to be reminded that he drifts into trouble so easily,' Madame Konstantine replied.

'Will you kindly stop talking about me as if I were a boy?' Petros complained easily. His smile had not slipped for a moment and April's blood was coming to a slow boil. So! She was piggy in the middle, was she?

'You *are* a boy when Michalis is around,' his sister intervened with a cheeky grin. 'When he is not around you are always in trouble. Marriage will sort you out.' Petros took a playfully threatening step towards her and she pulled a face before turning to April.

'I am Marika. I don't suppose either of them told you about me?'

'Oh, they did,' April managed pleasantly; at least that was only a part-lie. Petros had told her. There was no need to look as murderous as she felt at the moment. Marika seemed very nice. Her brothers were both villains!

'How astonishing. I am usually ignored. May I call you April? It's such a pretty name.'

'A pretty name for a pretty girl,' Petros said, his arm coming round April.

'A beautiful girl,' Michalis corrected, his eyes warning Petros and sliding over April coldly. 'She has not enjoyed the flight. I will take her to her room. You had better come too, *Mitera.*'

He took control, grasping April's arm and easing her away from Petros with no sign of the tight anger he was clearly feeling. And April didn't know about lying; for a man who scorned liars, Michalis was not doing too badly himself. She would have liked to be alone with him to point out this fact, but his mother came along and so did Marika.

Petros stayed back and April turned to glance at him with annoyance. He shrugged and held his hands out in a charmingly helpless way, a boyish smile on his face. She did not smile back; much more boyishness and she would spank him! She would have given anything for a few moments alone with them both.

Michalis tightened his grip and almost dragged her along. Nobody noticed because Marika was chattering away endlessly. April wondered if Petros had noticed. He was not going to get away with this. One tale to his mother, another to Michalis. What tale did he propose to tell her to get himself off the hook? Of course he might just not bother; momentarily she had forgotten that *she* was nothing!

It was another grand house, and April's heart sank a notch. Not that she had been expecting anything less than magnificence, but it was now hard to keep up her old defiant attitude even though her temper was soaring. She was entangled with lives that had nothing to do with her, and all because of an idealistic gesture that had forced her away from home, friends and safety.

She was also incredibly ensnared in the dark web of power and intrigue that Michalis had spun. It seemed to be all around her, tightening every time their eyes met, however she raged at him; and she was helpless here, unless she wanted to create a scene in front of his mother and make herself look cheap and foolish—an adventuress.

His mother was speaking now as they walked up the stairs to the bedrooms, and April had not heard a word she had said. She shot a look at Michalis and he simply raised one black brow, his mouth twisting in amusement. It must be all right. She was sure that if any answers had been needed *he* would have answered for her. She even knew that although he had called this his mother's house he was totally in control, and he was finding this situation extremely entertaining.

In the bedroom, Madame Konstantine began to show her where everything was—her bathroom, her veranda, the hairdrier—and Michalis just stood there silently, obviously waiting for the others to go. Marika sat on the bed, bouncing gently, keeping up a steady stream of comments that finally gained her mother's attention.

'Marika! It is not very polite to interrupt everything. Neither is it polite to bounce about on a guest's bed.'

Actually, April liked it. It made her feel less of an outsider. Marika seemed to be about nineteen, and she couldn't help comparing her open, pleasant ways with Gail. If Gail had been a little more like this then she would not have felt the need to leave home and come into danger. She might have looked a little more closely at the plea for help from Petros.

'April does not look as if she minds,' Marika pointed out cheerfully. 'In any case, she is not one of our stuffy guests. She is obviously Michalis's girlfriend, otherwise she would not have looked for Petros in England and taken care of him. She did it for Michalis because nobody in their right mind would seek out Petros unless they liked trouble. I have worked it all out for myself.'

'Now you may work yourself out of April's room,' Michalis ordered. 'I have already said she has not enjoyed the flight. She needs a little peace and quiet before lunchtime.' He was not denying anything at all, and April felt another wave of anxiety. She was getting more deeply into trouble all the time.

Marika did not exactly rush out, but she went, and so did Madame Konstantine with a rueful look in April's direction that was an apology for her daughter. It gave April the chance she needed.

'You've got some explaining to do,' she snapped in a low voice as they left. 'You've introduced another liar to the scene—*you*!'

'Merely for my mother's sake,' he said calmly, lifting her cases to the bed. 'You wish to unpack these at last? One of the maids will do it for you, of course. She will also press anything that requires it.'

'I don't wish to unpack!' April stormed quietly, his dismissive manner infuriating her. 'I've not unpacked so far and I'm not doing it now. You can call Petros up here and tackle him head-on. You know he's lying now even if you doubted it before. He joined in with another lie almost gleefully—your lie! Obviously he's addicted to lies.' She glared up at him. 'You're a funny family filled with obsessions—you with security and Petros with fantastic stories. There's a streak of insanity a mile wide and it goes straight through the male line, because it missed your sister. How she remains cheerful in the middle of so much derangement I can't think!'

She was breathless after her speech, and Michalis walked steadily towards her, his eyes narrowed and a half-smile of amusement on his face.

'Don't touch me!' April warned, holding her ground. They were not alone here and his mother was a very dignified woman. He was not going to reduce her to a trembling idiot again. He just kept on coming and she raised her head defiantly. 'I'll scream!'

He simply jerked her towards him, holding her shoulders tightly and staring down into her eyes ironically.

'Scream,' he invited. 'I will simply kiss it out of you.'

He wouldn't dare. The bedroom door was wide open and he had no idea where his mother was. April felt triumphant. She opened her mouth to scream, and instantly it was closed by his lips. She struggled fiercely but he held her fast, enclosing her in hard arms and lifting her closer still. Pushing against his shoulders was useless. It was like trying to move a wall, and his mouth was fused to hers with no hope of release.

She murmured anxiously, hurting with the pressure, and he relaxed his hold. His hand cupped her head and feelings of excitement began to pierce every part of her as his other hand slid down her back and closed around her hips, forcing her against him.

'Michalis!' She could even hear the trembling excitement in her own voice and his lips hardly left hers.

'Be quiet. You are being punished.' His hand slid down her slender thighs and then cupped her small, tight rear, crushing her against him as he explored her mouth heatedly. It was explicitly sexual, robbing April of any power to struggle further.

A sort of fluttering sound in the doorway had him lifting his head, but he lifted it lazily with no sort of worry. His mother was just disappearing round the corner, and April looked at him with frantic eyes, her expression still dazed.

'Now look what you've done,' she gasped unevenly. 'What will she think?'

'If I am not mistaken she will be smiling happily. I am thirty-six and long past the age when she thinks I should be married. She has a good business head and, like me, she does not feel easy about the fact that, should anything happen to me, Petros would be in charge of the family fortunes. She wants another Konstantine—a grandson.'

'How disappointed she's going to be,' April managed shakily. He smiled down at her arrogantly.

'She has been disappointed before. She has seen me with plenty of women. I am not a boy.'

'No. You're a toad!'

'A toad is a useful creature,' he remarked in amusement at her insult.

'I was thinking about slimy, dark and inhuman.'

'It cannot help it.' He was grinning down at her and he hadn't let her go either. She was still trapped, pressed close to the hard muscles of his body. He still had his hand in her hair and his fingers were moving subtly and deliberately, bringing the fire back.

'Let me go!' She was angry at his trick and angrier still with herself for feeling enchantment at the pressure of those hard lips.

But of course.' He moved his hands from her very slowly, stroking them over her. 'Do not scream, though. If you do, I think my mother will merely come up and shut the door. She will never believe anything now but burning passion. In any case, her hopes are too high.'

'I hate you!' April stormed. He had neatly removed her advantage and she knew it. She would have to scream the house down if she wanted any help. If his mother could make fluttery sounds and walk away from that passionate scene she must be desperate to get him married off. There had been no polite and outraged cough. What about Greek decorum now, then? She glared at him and shouted again. 'I hate you!'

'But of course you do,' he agreed silkily. 'I have kidnapped you and you have not yet become completely attached to your captor.'

'Will you please leave me to have this rest I need after my so-called bad flight?'

'Certainly, *despinis*. If you want anything let me know. I am at your beck and call—that is the correct expression, is it not?'

'Just you keep away from me,' April ordered uneasily, but he never replied. He was walking out with a very satisfied look about him that told her everything was going his way. It had all been managed so neatly, and now all he had to do was wait until the women were not there and force the truth out of Petros. She had the miserable feeling he wasn't going to find that easy. Petros now looked to be a very smooth customer to her. She would be taken ignominiously to her plane, some excuse given to his mother, and she would be branded permanently as a greedy, grasping seductress.

April went to get a shower. She had showered this morning but she was now very hot and bothered. It was impossible to be held close by Michalis and escape unscathed, and she had not escaped this time either. She could still smell the tangy aftershave. It lingered on her skin as if he were still kissing her, and if she was to face the battle to come she knew she had to put this magic right out of her mind. She had to stop thinking about those hard lips, those strong arms.

She told herself how much she hated him, how she was going to make him suffer, but she could still see his dark hair, dark eyes, the way his mouth quirked with ironic amusement. She stood under the shower and hoped it would all be washed away.

When she came back into her room, a maid was hanging up her clothes, some already put aside for pressing.

'Oh, I didn't want——'

'It is all right, *despinis*. Kyrios Konstantine ordered me to unpack for you. I will press these things.' The maid left the room, smiling pleasantly as if it was an honour, and April sat down to fume a little. He was invading every nook and cranny she had. She wasn't even allowed to have full suitcases any more!

At lunchtime she was glad, however. Marika and her mother had changed from casual clothes and sat down to eat in very expensive dresses. As her clothes had all been hanging up, April had changed too and was wearing one of her favourite things—a swirling dress of navy blue with small white flowers strewn across the skirt.

'Very demure,' Michalis murmured sardonically as he helped her to her chair. It was a sceptical remark meant for her ears alone. On the surface he was charming and certainly in control of the household—the master returned to his fortress.

When she looked up she was horrified to find Petros looking at her like a lovesick swain. It was all to fool Michalis, and it worked because as Michalis turned he noticed and his face was instantly like thunder. After that he only made any sort of polite conversation for his mother's sake. April suspected then that Petros intended to play this out to the end and her spirits fell a little more. She was securely trapped without even the freedom to shout out her annoyance.

Petros didn't have to wait long either. After lunch, Madame Konstantine wanted to speak to Michalis. She turned apologetically to April.

'I'm sorry, April, but when Michalis comes home it is necessary to go over so many things with him. I must get it done now. Tomorrow we are having guests, as you know, and, as head of the family, Michalis will be busy then. I won't keep him long.'

Obviously she had been quite taken in by the scene upstairs and, with Michalis watching her like a hawk,

April dared not say any of the tart things that sprang to her tongue.

'Oh, I can amuse myself, Madame Konstantine,' she managed sweetly.

'My dear, call me Lydia.' She patted April on the arm and then followed Michalis out to the study. The golden seal of approval! What would that charming woman think when she knew the whole truth? Because she would find out one day—April was sure of that. She looked around for Marika, but she had disappeared too and there was only Petros.

'Come along. I'll show you the gardens,' he said quickly when she turned sparkling eyes on him. 'I have to talk to you.'

'Talking is not going to get you out of this,' April muttered fiercely. 'The way I feel at the moment nothing short of your instant disintegration would do!'

'I can explain, April. Look, we can't talk here. I don't want Marika spying on us. She spends her life mixed up with other people's business.'

'She's not the only one,' April snapped. 'I'm mixed up in other people's business and it's not at all amusing.'

She let him lead her out into the garden, though. If she had to hit him it was as well to be out sight of more civilised people because she did not feel very civilised herself at the moment. If it hadn't been for Petros she would never have been anywhere near this mighty family. She would never have met Michalis either, and that would have been a very good thing!

'Why did you not come until today?' Petros demanded quickly as soon as they were away from the house. 'I've been waiting every day for you.' His attitude almost took April's breath away.

'I came several days ago,' she informed him angrily. 'In fact it feels as if I came several years ago.'

'What are you talking about?' He stopped by the tall flowering bushes and looked at her as if she should have a very good explanation.

'I'm talking about kidnapping, imprisonment and criminal charges when I get back home!' April announced furiously. 'Your lies to Michalis really went down well. He collected me in Athens and he's had me locked up ever since.'

'*Theos*! I might have known he would take action. He never gives one inch when his mind is made up. Battling with Michalis is like fighting a mountain.'

'What did you expect? And how dare you tell him that we stayed together at my flat, that we—we're lovers?'

'It just came into my head,' Petros confessed ruefully, that little-boy look on his face again. 'It was necessary and, in any case, I am tired of being ordered about. I have been ordered about all my life.'

'Perhaps you should have been *led* about, carefully tied up,' April snapped. 'Haven't you heard a word I said? Because of your lies I've been a prisoner at that— that house on the mainland.'

'How did I know he was going to do that?' Petros enquired with a hurt look that almost drove April to violence. 'I was just making plans of my own. I said it was necessary or I would not have done it. I needed your help. He controls every breath I take.'

'Let's hope he forgets one day. The breath you used to tell him about me has blackened my character. You can just go and find him and tell him the truth.'

'I can't,' he said urgently. 'I have to keep him on edge until the engagement dinner. I may not get the better of him but I must try. He has to sweat over this one. Help me, April.'

'He's not sweating,' April raged quietly. 'He's punishing me.'

'He will forget it later,' Petros assured her a little desperately. 'When I tell him the truth he will be filled with remorse, and Greek honour will ensure that you get a very nice gift from him.'

'You—you . . . !'

April was just about to explain to him exactly what he was when he suddenly grabbed her and pulled her close, burying his face in her hair. He had never held her before, and she was so startled that for a second she did not resist.

'April, darling,' he said wildly. 'Help me; how can I live without you? I have been thinking of you every minute since we parted. I cannot marry anyone else.'

'Get back to the house!' a voice ordered icily and April's heart sank like a stone. Michalis had come and Petros had seen him coming. That was the reason for this display of wild affection. How would she explain now?

'You can't separate us,' Petros said triumphantly. 'There's already too much between us. Nobody can take that away, and although I'm prepared to act out a lie for *Mitera's* sake I will not give April up!'

'Go!' Michalis looked capable of murder, and Petros went, leaving April to face the fury, the scorn and the certainty that was now in the midnight-black eyes.

'So!' He looked down at her coldly. 'You are a poor, misjudged girl, an innocent, a virgin. You were my brother's friend and nothing more. I can now see how skilful you really are at lies. For a while I was almost deceived.'

'I'm not lying!' April pleaded. 'He's doing it to get at you and for no other reason. He intends to get engaged. He doesn't want me. Go after him and ask him.'

'You imagine I need to ask him when I have just found you in his arms, heard him say he cannot live without you, will marry you and no one else? I do not need a picture drawing, *despinis*. I saw the whole scene in Technicolor!'

'You missed the beginning,' April reminded him desperately. 'He saw you coming.'

'But you did not. I noticed that you did not fight his embraces as you fight mine.'

She couldn't fight his for long—he was too much a fire to burn her to ashes—but April knew it was useless to go on arguing. He had made his mind up when he had first seen her, and now he was quite, quite certain. He just walked off and left her standing in the garden, and April knew she was now more branded than she had ever been.

As she began to follow in a forlorn way, his mother came out and Michalis stopped instantly. As yet, in this vast garden, Lydia Konstantine was some way off, and before she could come to join them Michalis turned to April and held out his hand.

'Come here!' he ordered, giving her a grim look that threatened instant reprisals if she refused. It wiped away April's misery and she stared at him bleakly.

'No way! I've now had enough, Mr Konstantine. Your days of tyranny are over. I'm about to speak to one of the sane members of your family. I intend to tell my story to your mother, and if she doesn't believe me then at least she'll insist that I be sent home.'

She was stunned at the speed of his reaction. A second before he had been standing waiting, a frown on his face;

now he was beside her, towering over her, his hands tightly on her arms.

'You would not dare!'

'Try me!' April glared up at him and it was her last voluntary action. He swept her up into his arms and walked down the garden towards the beach, away from the house, acting as if he had never seen his mother at all.

'Put me down!' April kicked her legs wildly, pummelling his chest with her fists, and as they came near the tall flowering bushes where she had recently had her annoying chat with his brother Michalis dropped her to her feet, grasping her face with hard hands, the bushes shielding them from sight.

'Scream and you know what will happen,' he threatened. 'Tomorrow my mother faces her future daughter-in-law. She is already worrying about arrangements, anxious for everything to be smooth and happy. If you even think about adding to her problems...'

'What about *my* problems?' April seethed.

'They are self-inflicted, and perhaps this time will be a good lesson to you that will last for the rest of your life. Whatever happens, I will not have my mother disturbed.'

'I should think she's pretty disturbed right now as we're behind the bushes like a couple of teenagers!' April snapped, struggling to get free.

'She thinks I am kissing you. She has already seen our devotion to each other. She will not intrude.'

'So much for Greek conventions!' April scoffed, but he looked down at her scathingly and smiled that nasty smile he sometimes had.

'The conventions exist and you will not break them by telling your plausible tales to my mother. As for me,

I am head of the family, which gives me some leeway. She will not, of course, expect you to behave as our girls behave. You are English.'

'And nothing!' April added bitterly.

He tilted his head on one side and looked at her critically as if he were about to sell her.

'You are useful at the moment,' he conceded. 'When your usefulness ends, I will take you to Athens and get rid of you.'

April opened her mouth to shout at him, and her intentions were plain in her angrily sparkling grey eyes. His threat was carried out without any waiting, his mouth covered hers instantly, and he kissed her into silence with no difficulty at all, pulling her tightly to him and crushing her rebellion with masterful ease.

'Do not look so devastated,' he ground out when she looked up at him with bewildered eyes. 'It is not too long ago that my brother kissed you in this very spot.' His eyes ran over her angrily, lingering on the tight swell of her breasts. 'Did he get the same reaction, or does your body save that for me?'

He took her hand and almost dragged her to the house. His mother had discreetly gone away and April wondered wildly how many other women he had brought here and kissed in front of his mother. What did he say? Go away, *Mitera*, I have some seduction to deal with? It wouldn't at all be beyond him. His arrogance was boundless.

In the hall he let her go, dropping her hand as if it disgusted him. It probably did, as he had scrupulous rules for other people. It was only for himself that he left a slack rein. April went to her room, rubbing a hand that now burned as much as her lips. Once again he had crushed all mutiny and she would have to work herself up to it before she could face his mother with any revelations.

She wasn't even sure if she could. Defying Michalis with her threats was one thing, sitting down to tell Madame Konstantine the whole tale was yet another. April had not forgotten the logic that Michalis had used when he had summed up his reasons for believing her a liar.

At the very best she would leave here under a cloud of disapproval. Quite a few people would be hurt, and it was not in April's nature to hurt anyone. Finally, of course, it would be Michalis who took her to the plane, and his actions since she had come here would prove that he too was lying to his mother. He might drop her out over the sea on the way to the mainland. She couldn't exactly put that past him.

CHAPTER SEVEN

APRIL stayed in her room. It seemed the wisest thing to do. There could be no escape attempts from here after all. The only way out of here was to tell Madame Konstantine everything, and after being seen twice in Michalis's arms April was too embarrassed to try that right now.

It was only early afternoon but she hoped they would all think she was tired. At least, if Marika Konstantine thought that then it would do. She didn't care at all what Michalis and Petros thought.

Michalis thought it unacceptable. He gave her an hour and then knocked on the door. When she let him in, he looked at her sternly.

'You are a guest of my mother. It is not possible to hide away here, no matter how much you wish to. You must come down and join the rest of the family. You may swim in the pool or simply sunbathe, but they are now worrying about you.' His lips tightened. 'Petros is particularly worried and it does not amuse me to have Marika asking where my girlfriend is.'

'Just tell them!' April sighed and turned away. 'You've made my life so complicated...'

'The complications belong to Petros and to you!' he grated. 'I have spoken to him and he has agreed to pretend that he knows you are with me. It removes one difficulty.'

'I *am* with you!' April turned on him in agitation. 'I'm your prisoner, and just think about Petros for a minute. If what he said were true, do you imagine he would be willing to pretend that I was with you? How is he going to explain that to everyone when the time comes?'

'There will be no explanations. You will go. Tomorrow this engagement will be finalised and then they will leave the next day for Athens where it will be celebrated and confirmed. You will leave too, for England.'

'You've got it all wrong, do you know that?' April said miserably. He was standing there, aloof and distant, completely inflexible, looking down his nose at her in his superior way, and she felt more trapped than she had felt at his house on the mainland. It didn't look as if Petros would confess now.

'I have not got it wrong. He repeated his words to me not half an hour ago,' Michalis informed her icily. She just turned away, feeling utterly desperate, covering her face with her hands.

'April!' Michalis strode forward and pulled her hands away. 'Stop that! You will get out of this in two days.'

'With my pride intact?' She looked up at him with glittering grey eyes, and his face took on a thoughtful, almost wary look, his mind probing into hers.

'I have tried to find out the truth,' he said quietly. He watched her for a minute and then gave an angry growl. '*Theos*! How can you look so innocent, so bewildered?'

'Because I am!'

His eyes stared into hers and then he turned away abruptly, letting her go.

'I wish you were,' he rasped. 'You have me so that I do not quite believe the evidence of my own eyes.' He walked out of the room and slammed the door and April settled down to a think. She just couldn't come up with an answer that would leave her feeling anything but cheap. If Michalis had not been able to kiss her into stupidity she would have told his mother and been out of this already. It was a little too late now.

She had pulled herself together, made up her face and was just about to go down to face everyone when a knock on the door had her almost running to answer. If only it was Michalis come to tell her that Petros had confessed.

It was Petros, and at the sight of him her face froze.

'That's far enough,' she said sharply. 'Don't try to take even one step into my room.'

'I've got to talk to you, April,' he said in an urgent, low voice. 'I owe you an explanation—the real one. I was trying to tell you out there in the garden, but Michalis seems to be everywhere at once. I'm sorry I had to pull that trick. Please let me talk to you and you'll understand.'

'I understand,' she told him bitterly. 'You explained before. You just want to get the better of Michalis and you don't care who gets hurt.'

'Yes. I want to get the better of him, but not how you think.' He looked at her ruefully. 'When I saw you earlier you had only just come, Michalis had not spoken to me, and I thought—well, I thought you were with him.'

'I was! I am!' April snapped, backing away and raising a warning hand when he tried to follow. She found she could be as imperious as Michalis when she wanted to be, and Petros stopped dead.

'I know. That is not what I meant. I saw you together and you looked so—so. . . He was looking at you as if he. . . I thought you were his woman!' he blurted out. 'You were days late in coming and he glared at me like a tiger guarding his mate. It altered my story to you because I thought you might tell Michalis and let me down.'

April was too stunned to really react. A tiger guarding his mate? A tiger guarding his kill would have sounded more believable.

'This time I'll tell you the truth,' Petros said quickly when she just stood and stared at him speechlessly. He was into the bedroom before she could summon up any further imperious signals. 'April! If you don't help me I'll lose the girl I love, the girl I want to marry.'

'I sincerely hope that's not me,' April muttered apprehensively, remembering his declaration that had finally convinced Michalis.

'I'm sorry but it is not,' he said with a smile. 'I have known who I would marry since childhood, and it has suited me fine. Stella is coming tomorrow. I have not seen her for weeks, but at one time she was always with me, my childhood friend and my sweetheart.' He laughed wryly. 'She was tactfully removed when our kisses were seen to be a little too warm. Her mother was slightly worried. Now she is to be mine at last. I will die if anything stops this, and so will she.'

'You're all mad in this house,' April declared, sitting on the bed and staring up at him. 'None of this makes sense. Just go ahead and get engaged to the girl. It's what everyone wants.'

'*Now* they do,' he told her urgently. He came and knelt down by the bed, looking at her seriously. 'There is something they do not know, however. Her family have lost almost all they have. Stella's father made several bad business ventures. They have never had the wealth that Michalis controls but they were fairly wealthy, acceptable. When the truth comes out everyone will know that they are not only poor but in debt. So far it has been kept quiet because Stella's mother is ill. It cannot be kept quiet for long, though. Michalis must know but he has said nothing.'

'He was too busy committing a crime,' April reminded him grimly. 'He had a kidnapping to do. What difference does this all make anyway? You don't have to marry for money. Just dig up a bag of gold for them.'

'I do not control anything. Michalis controls it. My mother always agrees with him. I have no one to turn to but you. Michalis may well be waiting until tomorrow to act. He will probably call it all off. He is head of the family and it will not be a suitable match. Our family always make suitable matches,' he added bitterly.

'Why hasn't he acted already?' April asked grimly. 'He behaves like the uncrowned head of Greece.'

'When you arrived he had another problem,' Petros pointed out. 'As you said, he was busy kidnapping you and he was also busy trying to make sure I did not marry you. You are not suitable either.'

April was beginning to feel sorry for Petros. His crimes were slipping from her mind. Her kind heart and fighting spirit could not accept this feudal way of carrying on. Michalis was suddenly looking like a villain again. A powerful villain who kidnapped innocent people and wrecked lives for money and snobbery.

'Look, Pete,' she said softly. 'I understand. What can I do, though? I'm not here of my own free will—not now anyway.'

'I know why you're here. I wanted you to come and pretend this, to help me, but I never got the chance to explain. Now I can't help by simply telling the truth. I'm to pretend that you're his girlfriend until the engagement is all over. That is for *Mitera's* sake, to explain your presence here when Stella comes. I've agreed, but

I protested and threatened, to keep him suspicious. April, just let it go on for another two days, please!'

'But why?'

'If he thinks I am intent on not marrying Stella because of you he will see to it that Stella and I are engaged with all speed, regardless of money. Otherwise there would be a scandal, you see. Too many people know about this. To reject a bride for reasons of money is quite suitable in this wealthy circle. To reject her for another woman is not. Michalis will do everything he can to shield my mother and to keep you and me apart.'

'And then what?' April was thinking rapidly. She could not be worse off, no matter what happened, so why not help Petros? It was a relief to know he did have a good reason for lying. Otherwise she would have felt very let down forever. She hadn't misjudged him after all.

'Then I will tell him,' Petros assured her vehemently. 'Two days, April, that is all. When Stella rang me and told me about her family troubles I was frantic because I knew what Michalis would do. Then I thought of you. I have been on edge ever since. I expected you to be brought straight here and I would have explained. I knew you were a good sport and I knew you would help me. I never imagined that Michalis would keep you locked up.'

April smiled ruefully. If she had come out here and been told she would have helped by pretending. It wasn't too late even now. It would also pay Michalis back soundly.

'OK. Count on me, Pete.' She made her mind up and grinned down at him. At least a fight would take her mind off those strong arms and burning lips.

'Oh, April! I knew you would. You're wonderful!' Petros grasped her round her knees and gave her a brotherly hug, and a voice from the open doorway cut like a white-hot knife into the scene.

'*Get out*!'

Michalis stood there like Zeus, ruler of the heavens. He seemed to be taller than ever, dark, and furious to the point of murder. His looks devastated April. At that moment he seemed all-powerful, invincible and frightening.

'April and I understand each other,' Petros said, and she had to admit that she admired him. Of course he had probably seen the chief god angry before. She hadn't. Once or twice she had imagined he was angry but she could see now that she had been mistaken; he had merely been mildly irritated.

'Go, before I forget who you are,' Michalis said in a deadly low voice. Petros glanced at April's pale and astonished face, and left, but not before he had patted her hand.

'Everything will be all right,' he said with a smile. It wasn't even a shaky smile. But then he was leaving; she was still here. He was doing all this for love and she was just a jolly good sport.

She just stared at Michalis with wide grey eyes, utterly hypnotised by his power, and he bunched his hands together in tight fists, fighting for constraint. When he spoke, the words came out in Greek at first. He had almost lost control and he was fighting to regain it. When he spoke in English, April flinched at the words.

'You deceitful little bitch! How many times have I looked at your face and questioned my own senses, my own judgement? I have even questioned the evidence of my own ears and eyes. Now my brother is here in your room, kneeling at your feet. What have you promised that makes him declare how wonderful you are? You will come back to Greece and be his mistress when he is married? You will go to him tonight?'

The insults stung April out of her hypnotic state and she didn't care if he *was* Zeus with the power to point a finger and throw lightning at her. She sprung to her feet and glared back at him.

'You toad!' she shouted. 'You black, slimy, money-grabbing toad!'

He was inside the room in one stride, the door slammed shut, but April ran round the bed, giving herself plenty of room for manoeuvre.

'This time I'll really scream,' she warned furiously. 'This time I'll scream and scream until the whole household arrives here, and I'll tell the lot of them, but it won't be the tale you've heard so far. I've got a much better one.'

Michalis looked at her with icy, narrowed eyes, not moving a step forward. His face was like polished rock, cold, handsome and utterly still. Only the carved lips moved.

'I shut the door to save myself the embarrassment of explaining your raised voice,' he said coldly. 'I have no intention of touching you again, Miss Stewart. I do not want my brother's woman.'

He walked out, closing the door with controlled violence, and April collapsed on to the bed. She felt as if she had just met the most powerful man in the world, the most furious one. For a second she had been in ancient Greece and it had scared her. Two days. She would play it out. Michalis was not a god after all, unless he was the god of greed.

*   *   *

When she went down he was nowhere to be seen. She sat by the pool watching Marika swim, and Petros came to sit beside her.

'I am sorry about that, April,' he said in a low voice.

'It worked,' she pointed out, looking down the garden to avoid his eyes. She didn't want Petros to see the misery in hers. 'If he doubted any intrigue he certainly believes it now. In any case, it gave me a good excuse to give him a piece of my mind.'

'I have never seen him so wildly angry,' Petros muttered, staring into the pool but obviously thinking of the near-violence on his brother's face.

'Really? I thought it was normal,' April said bleakly. 'Good old Greek drama.'

'Greeks laugh readily,' he assured her with a wry grin. 'Michalis as much as anyone. He is normally understanding too. I have been in many scrapes in my life and as often as not he has rescued me with little more than a stern reprimand.'

'Well, now you have two girlfriends at a very delicate time,' April reminded him. 'It makes a difference.'

'Even that would normally have brought only an acidly delivered lecture and a speedy smoothing-over. Michalis and I have always been close. He is my big brother. I thought for a moment he was going to kill me. I have never seen him like that—so close to losing his self-control.' He turned to her with a puzzled look. 'Why did he not put you on a plane instead of bringing you here today? He knew that Stella was coming tomorrow and after that the family is going to Athens. He could have told me you had not arrived and it would have been too late then.'

'He wanted to know who was lying,' April said bitterly. 'I don't think he could accept the fact that it might be you. I didn't take to captivity very well. I gave him a lot of trouble. Finally I think he began to wonder if I was telling the truth.' She didn't want to think about the time when Michalis had decided to bring her here—the night with his arms around her, the night when she had almost belonged to him.

'I have lied before,' Petros confessed, and April looked at him ruefully.

'I can imagine! All the same, you're his brother and he would not want to take my word before yours. I can see he had to find out. I'm nothing after all—just an English pauper with a temper. Pride wouldn't allow him to leave it at that. He's much more comfortable in his mind now he really believes you.'

'I wonder.' Petros gave her a long look and then stood. 'I had better not be near you when Michalis appears. That rage might still be on the boil. I do not think he could have controlled it earlier even if *Mitera* had been there.'

Neither did April, and she was glad seconds later that Petros had moved because Michalis came out and dropped down into a seat beside her. Petros was now in the pool, splashing Marika, and Michalis stared at them in sombre silence. April glanced at him secretly. He was still in a rage. His lips were one straight line, his eyes narrowed against the sunlight on the water of the swimming-pool. He wasn't looking at his brother with any sort of speculation, though. He finally believed it all completely.

In white jeans and black shirt he looked as magnificent as any man could look, and April turned away rather frantically as shivers ran over her skin. He had warned her that people became attached to their captives. It was sneaking up on her too.

She closed her eyes, trying to get the sight of him out of her mind, and she never heard his mother come out.

'April? Are you all right?'

Lydia Konstantine's soft voice had April opening her eyes quickly and she found the older woman standing beside her, looking down at her a little worriedly. Michalis too was sitting upright, staring at her, his brow furrowed in a deep frown.

'Oh, yes,' she managed faintly. 'I was just closing my eyes against the glare of the water.'

'You are quite pale,' Lydia pointed out with a certain amount of disquiet.

'I—I have a headache, actually,' April confessed. 'I've had a couple of—of unusual days and I don't expect I'm used to so much excitement. Maybe it's a cold coming on.'

'I could get you a tablet,' Lydia offered.

'No, thank you. I have some of my own, and if it gets any worse I'll take a couple. Please don't worry about me. I'll be all right.' April smiled up at Lydia and at that moment a maid came out to speak to her. As his mother went, Michalis continued to stare at April.

'On the cliff-top you were soaked to the skin.'

'So were you,' April muttered, avoiding his eyes.

'I have a little more muscle than you,' he pointed out irritably. 'I do not go down with colds at the first sign of rain.'

'Neither do I. In any case, it was my own fault.'

'It was *my* fault!' Michalis bit out in a low, savage voice. 'And all to no avail. Now we have another lie to live out!'

April jumped up to go. She could no longer bear this violent dislike, but his hand closed around her wrist tightly.

'Sit down!' he rasped. 'You are with me, remember? If you are ill, I will take care of you with the assistance of my mother. I do not wish to find Petros in your room, bathing your head and comforting you.'

Tears of self-pity threatened but she stifled them as Marika climbed out of the pool and sat on the marble surround almost at their feet, water dripping from her long hair.

'Quarrelling?' she asked with a sly grin. 'I have never heard a lovers' quarrel. May I listen?' Michalis looked as if he was about to lift her and drop her into the pool on her head, and April intervened quickly.

'We were not quarrelling. I have a headache and Michalis was blaming himself. I got wet at—at . . .'

'At his house on the cliffs?' Marika asked with a grin as April's voice trailed away at this mistake. 'I wondered if you had been there. Now *I* am not allowed to go any-where alone. I would not be allowed to be alone with a man. Michalis thinks I am a child.'

'And you are now proving it with your insolent chatter!' Michalis snapped. 'If I imagined for one minute that you were attempting to insult April . . . !'

'Oh, I am not!' Marika blushed and looked dismayed. 'Please, April, I was not even thinking about it. I was being impossible as usual.' She looked tearful herself and April smiled down at her.

'I'm not insulted,' she assured her. 'I'm a good five years older than you and quite able to take care of myself and, in any case, there were servants, as you know. Believe me, I don't find you impossible. I have a new stepsister with much more impossible tendencies. However, she's only seventeen. With any luck, she'll grow out of it.'

'Do you have to live with her?' Marika asked seriously, obviously shocked at the idea of living with anyone worse than herself.

'No, I have my own flat. When I get back home I should think she may have mellowed a bit.' April's voice was rueful and Marika was about to ask more, but a glance at Michalis had her changing her mind.

'Would it be all right to ask what you do for a living?' she asked a bit tentatively, looking warily at Michalis from the corner of her eye. April laughed and nodded.

'Perfectly all right. I do interior designing for people. They call me to their houses to see what the place needs and I come up with plans and then alter it—if they can afford it.'

'Will you explain it all to me?' Marika asked, preparing to settle down in the sun and have a good long talk. Michalis put a stop to it.

'When she has recovered from her headache and from the trauma of this interrogation,' he said firmly. 'Right now, she is going to take her tablets and lie down until dinnertime.'

'When I have a boyfriend he will not order me about,' Marika promised, lying back and closing her eyes against the sun.

'You will probably never have a boyfriend,' Michalis said drily. 'I will have to buy you a husband when the time comes, unless we can find a man who is deaf.'

Marika scooped up water from the pool with great speed and tossed it over him, wetting his white jeans. She was not afraid of her brother. April stood amazed at this swift retaliation, a burst of alarm flooding over her as he scooped up his sister with equal speed and dropped her into the pool. A wild burst of Greek insults were flung at him from the safety of the water, but he just stood and grinned down at his sister.

'Punish him, April!' Marika spluttered. 'Hit him for me!'

April managed a smile but her heart was very heavy. She had never seen Michalis like this before—a big brother with all the authority of the head of the family but all the threatening playfulness of a lifetime of caring. She remembered the words that Petros had said too. No matter how cold Michalis was with her, he loved his family. She didn't understand Greek ways anyhow.

'I will get a maid to bring you some iced water,' Michalis said briefly as they entered the cooler house. 'It would be as well to rest before dinner.' He just walked off and left her, and she stared after him. She was dismissed, cut off, to be ignored unless his family were watching. He had categorised her now and he had no further doubts.

The headache was very real and she wasn't surprised. In this time with Michalis she seemed to have lived a lifetime, most of it dramatic. She took her tablets, curled up in her dressing-gown on top of the bed, and went to sleep. Sleeping was a good idea; it passed the time, every minute bringing her closer to escape. He would put her on a plane and then stride off to take up his important life as if she had never even existed. She told herself that she didn't care. She would get over these blows to her pride.

April went on sleeping. She never heard Lydia Konstantine come into her room and look down at her worriedly. She had no idea how pale she looked, how the shadows under her eyes showed faintly purple beneath her thickly curling dark lashes. It was only as Michalis came in and stood looking at her that she stirred, and then only slightly, murmuring and distressed in her sleep.

'April.' He spoke her name quietly and then shook her shoulder. 'April.' She opened her eyes then, slightly disorientated, still aware of the headache, her face tensing as she looked up at him. He looked serious and moody and she tried to struggle up.

'What is it?' Her grey eyes narrowed in pain and he did not miss the fact.

'*Mitera* came to wake you for dinner. She was worried after seeing you. Your head is still bad?'

'Yes,' she confessed, 'but it doesn't matter. I'll get ready.'

'No. Stay where you are.' His hand restrained her as she tried to get up. 'If you come down looking so pale she will only worry. One of the maids will bring your dinner on a tray.'

'I won't worry her,' April said wearily. 'Do you think I've done this deliberately to annoy you? If you'd rather I stayed here I will, but don't say it's for your mother. I know you can't stand the sight of me. Well, you shouldn't have kidnapped me in the first place and then you wouldn't have to see me!' Tears came to her eyes and he looked down at her violently.

'It is not because I cannot stand the sight of you!' he gritted through clenched white teeth. 'It is because you look ill and pale. I am trying to be kind yet again. What do you want me to do, stay here and comfort you? Lie on the bed with you and kiss you better? I cannot do that, can I? You already belong to my brother!'

She wanted to scream that it was not true, but now she had promised Petros, and it made no difference in any case. Michalis despised her. She was not one of this mighty clan. For a few mad moments he had wanted her, but he would have forgotten her already if she had not been here, right under his nose, infuriating him. She closed her eyes and turned away, and he strode from the room with the savage energy she was so used to.

Petros stole up to see her after dinner, and she looked at him uneasily as he stood in the doorway.

'Please don't come in, Pete,' she begged worriedly. 'At the moment I don't think I could stand another burst of rage from your brother. Just let my head get better and I'll be in a more fighting spirit.'

'I just wanted to see if you're all right,' he assured her, looking at her gloomily. 'This is all my fault. Looking back, I can see the utter madness of it. At the time it seemed just a way of solving the problem without anyone being hurt. I never even thought of Michalis meeting you. I told him when he was here and he said nothing—well, nothing pleasant. He was going back to the mainland and when he got there he rang and said he would meet you. There wasn't a lot I could do. He never sent the helicopter back and it was too late to go by boat. When I rang he told me you hadn't come.'

'You didn't ring for couple of days,' April reminded him drily.

'I know. As a matter of fact, I dared not.' He shrugged angrily. 'I know it makes me sound like a scoundrel but I thought if he had met you he would instantly believe that I was lying. I just didn't want to know.'

'Why should he believe me?' April asked. 'He's your brother.'

'I do not have your innocent looks,' Petros assured her ruefully. 'I assumed that one look at you and Michalis would know who was lying.'

'You underestimate me. One look at me and he assumed I was an adventuress.'

'*You*? Oh, April, you look full of fun and fire, but there's a light in those shining grey eyes that would hold any man off.'

'Thanks. It's the urge to kill.'

'It's innocence, April. Even if there had been no Stella, I would have circled you warily.'

'Which would have been as well,' April retorted. 'I'll pick my own man.'

'You have already done that, have you not?' he asked softly. 'It is Michalis.'

'Now I'm *quite* sure the men in this family are mad,' April snapped, lying down and drawing the cover over her, declaring the interview over.

'Perhaps,' he mused thoughtfully. 'All I know is that you look very unhappy and Michalis is downstairs looking like death—and thunder.'

'I'm not surprised,' April mumbled from beneath the sheets. 'He's probably wondering which one of us to kill.'

'I think it would be me,' Petros assured her quietly, smiling apologetically at the crown of her shining hair, the only part of her he could see. 'If it would solve his problem I think he would give great consideration to it.' He went out and closed the door but April did not surface.

She knew why Michalis was so thunderous. He had the problem of trusting her. Tomorrow, Stella would arrive and it would be a solemn Greek occasion. Serious arrangements would be made. He would be wondering what she would do—if she would suddenly tire of obeying him and blurt out the truth. He would be imagining that she might rush to his brother's side and cling to him.

He had taken a great risk in bringing her here, and all to find out the truth. He still did not know the truth, and even if he did he would simply breathe a sigh of relief and get rid of her. Two days and Petros was safe with his Stella. What did it matter to her? Nothing! She most certainly had not chosen Michalis!

All the same, she went to sleep unhappy and never heard Michalis come in much later to stand and look down at her shadowed eyes and her pale cheeks. She never heard him leave either, his eyes black and empty, his face tight with control.

CHAPTER EIGHT

THEY came in the middle of the morning, arriving in the Konstantine helicopter. It touched down on the lawn as it had done when it brought April with Michalis, the hot sunlight glittering on the silver sides of the machine and making it impossible to see who was there at the windows.

Everyone waited, and this time April waited with them. She had recovered from her tense headache and come down to breakfast, feeling guilty when everyone greeted her warmly—everyone, that was, but Michalis. Even in front of his mother and sister he was finding it difficult to be normal with her—at least to be as normal as he was supposed to be with a girlfriend.

April did not know if Lydia noticed, but if she did she made no comment. Petros and Marika certainly noticed. Marika kept silent, with none of her usual chatter. Petros smiled at her apologetically. He knew of course that this day was very significant. If all went well, Michalis could be told tomorrow, and April was not looking forward to it. After all, he had been deceived and his proud nature would not accept that any more than it would accept the romance that he assumed was between April and his brother.

When they went forward to greet Stella Martis and her father, April hung back. She had nothing to do with this except in a sacrificial way. Petros looked tense and when he glanced at her she smiled and nodded, assuring him it would be all right. He smiled back, winking at

135

her. Everything depended upon today, and their eyes met in conspiracy.

Unfortunately, Michalis saw the little exchange of signals and his tight face tightened even further.

'You will come with us to greet them,' he grated in a low voice, taking her arm and urging her forward, almost pushing her in front of him.

'I'm not family,' April protested. 'I'll feel awkward and embarrassed.'

'You mean you will have difficulty keeping your dismay from showing when you see Stella?' he asked savagely. 'You will never be family but it does not exclude politeness. And remember, too, when you are tempted to speak out, England is far away.'

Words of protest sprang to her lips but she bit them back. The time for pleading was past and he would not listen in any case; he had never listened. His opinion of her was fixed, never to be altered. He had made his mind up about her on sight.

'Very well,' she said bleakly, allowing him to urge her towards the guests. 'It doesn't matter after all, does it? Tomorrow they go and so do I. You made your mind up about me the moment you saw me.'

'Yes!' he rasped. 'I wanted you!'

The ferocity with which he said it, made even more dramatic because his voice was low and dark, had April's legs trembling immediately. She went like someone in a daze, almost floating at his side, not really seeing anything. Sometimes he had a way of enveloping them in sensation as if nobody else existed. He could set her senses swimming with a word, a look, and his anger didn't seem to matter.

'You are with me!' he bit out and she nodded like a slave.

'I know.' It was chemistry, the hold he had on her magical, in spite of everything. Something had happened to her that she had never known existed and it would always colour her days. Meeting Michalis had been the best thing and the worst thing in her life.

A tall, elderly man stepped down from the helicopter and reached up for the girl who now appeared in the sunlight. She was dark, small, her wide dark eyes a trifle anxious, but as she saw Petros a smile lit up her face. She was not a beautiful girl, but she was so pretty, so fresh-looking that April smiled too. The sacrifice was worth it after all. She was doing her bit for true love and she only had to see Petros to know that. He was glowing with pride and joy.

'Look at him,' Michalis growled. 'Do you still think I am forcing him into this? A man does not look at a woman like that unless he cares very deeply. He has always cared, always cared, always been like that with Stella. For a while you drove him to madness but she will make him sane again.'

April never replied. Nobody could drive Michalis to madness; certainly she could not. She repeated in her mind the small litany that kept her going—Just until tomorrow. After tomorrow she would be away from all this, away from the glamour, away from the intrigue.

She was included in the flurry of greetings, and Stella smiled warmly as they shook hands. There was no sign of anxiety at this extra guest. She was sure of Petros; they were looking at each other with complete understanding. Her father, though, seemed a little put out, glancing quickly at his future son-in-law, and Lydia Konstantine picked it up at once.

'It is a little unusual to have another guest at a family occasion like this,' she said smoothly, 'but April knows both my sons. She is here for a holiday.'

'And she belongs to me,' Michalis intervened firmly. His arm came round April, pulling her to his side, and Stella's father visibly relaxed. April could understand why. He must be very much on edge himself at the moment. One word out of place and this betrothal would be cancelled. She even felt the agitation herself and wanted to rush them inside to get things settled and finalised. If anything happened now her sacrifice would have been for nothing and she knew she would not then be able to hold her tongue. She could imagine the embarrassment and the fury that would follow.

Back in the house, nothing happened at all. It was all stately, almost regal, the polite conversation making her more and more on edge. Her eyes met Stella's and the Greek girl smiled. April didn't know how she was living through it. She wanted to take her aside and tell her to hurry things up, and her agitation must have shown clearly because Petros collected Stella and drifted over to April almost unnoticed by the others.

'I have told her,' he said softly.

'But how . . . ?' April looked at them anxiously and Petros turned so that her face was hidden from the rest of the family.

'The usual method. The telephone. We are allowed to communicate even though we are not allowed to be alone at the moment. Try not to look so desperate, April. Michalis will notice and we have almost made it to the end of this.'

'How can we thank you?' Stella said in a sort of awe-stricken voice. 'Why are you doing this for us, April?'

'Well, it seemed so unfair, so disgraceful, and anyway, why not? I have nothing to lose and I like a good fight.'

'If Michalis finds out you will get one—so will we,' Stella pointed out, glancing round anxiously.

'He is not going to find out,' Petros soothed, gently touching her face. 'He will be kept on edge until it is finalised. I am very good at acting and April has a tongue as swift as my brother's temper. Whatever he knows about your father's problems, April is a much bigger problem.'

'He is watching us,' Stella whispered.

'Good. He will be furious and suspicious but there is nothing he can do.' Petros looked quite sure of this but he was wrong. Michalis came over and draped his arm around April's trembling shoulders.

'This seems to be a very secret conversation.' His voice was deceptively indulgent but his arm was almost cruel around her.

'We have been explaining to Stella how we met,' Petros lied. 'However, we had not managed to get very far with our explanations.'

'They will have to wait until later, I fear,' Michalis pointed out. 'Lunch is about to be served.'

He did not leave April to make any mischief. He took her hand and led her away, making for the dining-room and the others. He never asked what had been said either, but he looked closely at Stella, and April had to give her full marks for anxiety, a trembling smile and puzzled eyes. It did nothing to smooth things over. Michalis was quietly angry and as watchful as a hawk. He too wanted things settled, and for very different reasons. If it hadn't been so heart-breaking, April would have laughed aloud.

During the meal Stella's father informed them apologetically that his wife had been too ill to travel.

'She is not very strong,' he murmured. 'Tomorrow, though, she will be able to join us. The flight would have been too much for her.'

'I have had the yacht brought into harbour,' Michalis announced. 'I thought it would be very well worth a party of some size. The day after tomorrow we will really celebrate this engagement. I hope Madame Martis will be well by then.'

'You never told me, Michalis,' Lydia Konstantine pointed out in surprise.

'I do not tell you everything, *Mitera*.' He smiled at her gently. 'I thought it appropriate. Your youngest son is to be married. Surely you want all Greece to know?'

'Will the fairy lights be on the mast, Michalis? Will there be an orchestra?' Marika's excited questions brought smiles to everyone and Michalis was no exception.

'It will light up the night,' he promised indulgently. 'You will wear your very best dress and become a princess.'

'It is so exciting! Did you bring a very splendid dress with you, April?' Marika asked eagerly. 'When Michalis brings his yacht in it is really a very big occasion.'

'Oh, I won't...' April began, but strong, warning fingers covered her hand as it lay on the white cloth of the table.

'If she has not brought a splendid dress there is time to get one,' he said firmly. 'I will take her to the shops tomorrow afternoon.'

'I'll come with you,' Marika announced, and once more Michalis stepped into the awkward gap.

'Perhaps. We will see,' he said with finality as April looked a bit wild-eyed and Petros looked extremely puzzled What plans was Michalis making now? Did she have to stay and see this thing out even further? Was this cruelty to punish her, to make her see that she did not belong here at all? She could not look at anyone when he released her trembling hand and when her eyes met those of Petros across the dining table he was beginning to look worried. She knew he was worried for her now. He knew his powerful brother. Nobody played tricks on Michalis Konstantine—not if they wished to survive.

After lunch the tension increased because Mr Martis suddenly asked to speak to Michalis privately. It was not only April who was surprised—even Petros had not expected this, and neither had Stella. Nobody seemed to know what to do as they waited, and Marika took April's arm, dragging her out into the sunlit area around the pool.

'Now what is happening?' she muttered. 'I have never been mixed up in any betrothal arrangement before. It is nerve-racking. At any moment I am expecting people to shout and argue. What comes next, April?'

'Don't ask me. In England most people just walk in one day and announce that they are engaged.'

'Really? And then what happens?'

'Well, everyone is pleased and offers congratulations. They pretend to be pleased even if they're not. It really is nobody's business except the couple involved. If they're happy, most people have the sense to leave them to it.'

'That sounds good,' Marika mused. 'I would probably like that—although,' she added slowly, 'I think I would prefer it if Michalis approved.'

April smiled to herself. She could just imagine Marika waltzing in and announcing that she was engaged without prior approval. Michalis would probably look at her with

hard eyes and say, 'Oh, no you are not!' It would have
to be some carefully chosen young man. It made her
realise yet again how very much apart from Michalis she
was, how ordinary. She was all right to desire but nothing
more.

She stayed outside with Marika when everyone else
had their little gathering. She had been surprised to see
Mr Martis come from his meeting with Michalis with a
very relieved air about him, and his lessened tension
made everyone else relax. The trick had obviously
worked. Anything was better than having Petros marry
a penniless English girl.

'Well, they are not quarrelling,' Marika noted. 'Now
we can get it over and return to normal. The maids have
rooms ready for Stella and her father. Tomorrow
morning we are all flying to Athens. It will mean at least
two trips with the helicopter, unless Michalis has ordered another one out here. Don't go wandering off with
Michalis, will you, April? I want to go with you for your
dress.'

She never seemed to notice that April said nothing to
that. As usual she was chattering, and soon her attention returned to April's job. She wanted to know all
about it and it passed quite a lot of time.

'Why is your stepsister awful?' she finally enquired in
her usual forthright manner.

'She's not really awful,' April mused, looking out at
the garden. 'I can understand. I feel sorry for her. It's
because she's so insecure. A long time ago her mother
walked out and left them. Then there was a divorce last
year. For years Gail has lived with her father, and she's
only seventeen. He's been everything to her and she
doesn't want to share him. She's also had to give up her
home. The house has gone as part of the divorce

settlement and so she's not only got a new stepmother and stepsister, she's moving into our house, alien territory.'

'Does she dislike you?' Marika asked, spinning round to look closely at April.

'I think so. Never mind, I'm working on it. I have my own flat and when they went on their honeymoon I decorated the whole house and made a great deal of fuss about Gail's room. I wanted it to look like another place, new for all of them. That way she'll feel more at home there than I do. She'll certainly be in it before I can even visit. By the time I get back home, Gail will be more settled. I'll be more of the outsider. It will give her an advantage.'

'An advantage over you? Why are you so kind to her?'

'She's hurting,' April said softly. 'I understand.'

'You're a very kind person, April. You have given all the time and effort. I hope she appreciates it.'

'So do I,' April murmured wryly. 'I just about emptied my bank account doing it,' she added thoughtlessly.

'Michalis will buy your dress,' Marika announced, flinging herself back into the chair with her usual abandon. 'He has more wealth than even I can imagine, and you deserve it. It is like a fairy-tale—the kind, gentle princess and the rich, gallant knight.'

'The poor, penniless princess and the bad-tempered knight,' April corrected with a laugh. When she looked up, the bad-tempered knight was standing quite close by and watching them intently. His eyes held April's and he studied her face for a long time before he spoke.

'It is all arranged,' he informed her quietly. 'Come for a walk on the beach. I have done my duty and now there is only tomorrow.'

April knew that. She stood without demur and walked towards him.

'Can I come with you?' Marika asked, opening her eyes and looking at them slyly.

'No,' Michalis said uncompromisingly. 'It is not for children.'

'I am nineteen!' Marika said indignantly. 'April says that in England people just get engaged without permission. I will probably do that.'

'But who will have you, baby sister?' Michalis asked with silky teasing. 'I have told you. You will need a lot of help to trap a husband. You will also need coaching in diplomacy. No man wishes to marry a woman who cannot hold her tongue at least some of the time.'

'I think April probably speaks up for herself,' Marika said huffily. 'Still,' she added with a sigh, 'she is kind and gentle. I will have to learn from her.'

Michalis said nothing. He just took April's arm and led her down the garden towards the beach. He never spoke and it was perhaps as well. If he spoke he would say something to hurt her, and being who she was she would answer back. It was better to be silent; that way she could pretend. In any case, it was nearly over.

He said nothing until they stood at the end of the garden, looking out to the sea, the lawn sloping gently to the sand.

'It is done,' he said quietly. 'Everything is over and now there is nothing you can do.'

'I never intended to do anything.' April walked away slowly, coming down to the sand and stepping into the yielding softness. She took off her sandals and let them swing from her hand as she walked away from him.

Yes, everything was over. There was tomorrow, some sort of ceremony she supposed, and then when they were all on the yacht—friends, relatives gathered to dance and dine—she would be on her way back to England. She would never see the great yacht that Marika had described. She would never see the darkness lit up by the coloured lights, the candles and the glitter of beautiful gowns. It was as well. She would be totally out of place there.

Michalis caught her and swung her to face him, looking down at her vibrantly. He just stared at her, his face filled with frustration.

'Why can I not understand you?' he asked impatiently. 'How can you be two people at the same time? I look at you and see an innocent and yet you came here to continue an affair with Petros. I see a sweet, gentle face and yet you chased after him for wealth.'

'How do you know?' April asked carefully, glancing up. 'Maybe I'm mad about him.'

'You treat him like a mother,' he muttered frustratedly. 'I have watched you, seen you with him, heard your tone, and it is not passionate. Your breath does not catch in your throat. It is all you can do not to pat him on the head!'

'I'm playing a part,' April informed him, trying to turn away. 'You threatened what would happen if I didn't.'

'You play the part better than you play the reality. When I touch you, you are not acting. You tremble and your cheeks flush like a wild rose. I could take you at any time and you would not resist; you have never resisted.'

She looked at him anxiously and he turned away with an angry sound in his throat.

'I am not about to put it to the test,' he growled. 'I just wonder how far your lying goes. You have no money because you gave it away, made a new home for a step-sister who dislikes you. Is that why you had to come to Greece? Did you come for no other reason than to let her take your home from you?'

'You—you were listening to a private conversation,' April stammered, avoiding his eyes. 'In any case, it's a different thing. I came here to be with Petros. I—I came here to get him for myself.'

'Did you?' he muttered, pulling her to face him. 'Did you, April?' He tilted her downcast face and stared into her eyes. 'Shall I keep you here until I know every last bit of the truth? Shall I keep my prisoner until she confesses everything?'

'You—you couldn't! Your mother would know and I...'

'And what?' he asked softly. 'You would escape? You did not manage it before and there is still the house on the cliffs. There we would be alone with just Georgios and Sofia. Who would know that I still had you with me?' He was staring into her eyes again, she was looking back as helplessly as she had ever done, and he smiled darkly. 'Am I hypnotising you now, April? Shall I snap my fingers later and just have you follow me? Shall I keep you under a spell until you come to my bed?'

'I—I'm not—not innocent,' April whispered, unable to look away. 'There's Petros.' Her mind was frantically asking her why she was deepening the lie when it was almost time to confront him, but she was not in control of her mind; Michalis controlled it.

'Is there?' he asked softly. 'Is there Petros?' He pulled her into his arms, wrapping her close to him, his hand keeping her face tilted to his. 'Are you thinking of Petros now? Or are you thinking of me?'

The lips she had thought would never meet her own again closed over her mouth and he tightened her to him as his fingers threaded into her hair. He had been questioning, taunting, but now he was suddenly not playing with her emotions any more. His arm tightened and he lifted her off her feet, his mouth moving over hers compulsively until she let her arms float around his neck and just gave in. It was all there would ever be, and she would remember this.

She felt her feet gently touch the sand and he raised his head, looking down at her. She was trembling, bewildered, her grey eyes clear and bewitched and he made a low, impatient sound.

'You asked me once if you looked like a seductress and I said no,' he muttered frustratedly. 'You still do not. Tell me the truth, April. Tell me before it is too late.'

Alarm bells rang and she came out of her daze. What did he know? What did he suspect? Was it still not too late to draw back from this engagement? It was a risk she could not take.

'I—I've told you the truth,' she whispered.

'So why do I doubt it?' He let her go but held on to her hand, leading her back to the house. 'You *will* tell me the truth,' he said quietly. 'Tomorrow they leave. I have to be with them, but that plane is still not a certainty, *despinis*. Many things can happen before you see England again.'

If it was supposed to frighten her, it did not. If he was threatening to keep her, the thought made her suddenly happy, no matter what happened later.

His announcement at dinner made shivers run down her spine.

'The helicopter will only take three,' he reminded everyone. 'It will arrive in the morning for Kyrios Martis and Stella. *Mitera*, I think you should leave with them.'

Madame Konstantine nodded her agreement and then he turned to Petros.

'You can leave on the next flight with Marika and deliver her to Athens and the safekeeping of *Mitera*.'

'But what about April?' Marika asked indignantly. 'I want to go with her for the dress.'

'The second run cannot take all of us and our various belongings,' Michalis pointed out reasonably, 'unless of course you are proposing to leave me behind and carry on without me? I will bring April on the last flight.'

'It will be late,' Marika protested.

'It is not a million miles. I have ordered the first flight for ten in the morning.'

'You could have had more than one helicopter and——' Marika began, but Madame Konstantine shushed her in embarrassment and Michalis fixed her with amused eyes.

'Remember what I said about your need for coaching, little sister,' he warned. 'Kyrios Martis will be astounded at your impudence.'

'I know Marika,' Stella's father said with a wide smile, a smile that had seemed to grow more as the day progressed. 'She is a breath of fresh air.'

'A very strong breath at times,' Michalis corrected drily. 'The breath of fresh air is sometimes almost a whirlwind.'

It silenced Marika and she sat very guiltily for the rest of the meal. It did not amuse her nineteen-year-old dignity to have everyone grinning at her.

'In future I shall keep absolutely silent,' she told April later as they took coffee on the patio with the stars wild and high above them.

'Don't do anything of the sort,' April advised. 'Stick up for yourself.'

'Oh, I hope Michalis marries you,' Marika sighed. 'You would be such a comfort to me, such a wonderful ally.'

April didn't have to answer that one because she suddenly found herself the centre of attraction. Stella and Petros wanted to talk to her, Lydia Konstantine wanted to tell her where to shop for a dress and Stella's father wanted to speak about England, a place he had never visited.

Michalis just sat watching, his eyes thoughtfully on her, and when later his mother declared that it was too cold to just sit outside and suggested that they all go to the *sala*, April was glad to be able to avoid the dark eyes that had watched her so relentlessly.

He took her arm and held her back as the others moved inside, and she looked up at him anxiously as he kept her in the darkness.

'Do not look at me like that,' he growled impatiently. 'I am not about to beat you.'

'I never expected that you were,' she said quietly. 'What I expect from you is harsh words and hurt.'

'Hurt? I can hurt you, *despinis*?' He moved further into the darkness, taking her with him. 'I remember that you promised me great trouble, imprisonment and notoriety. You were never afraid, were you? You were simply enraged.'

'Outraged,' April corrected tartly. 'It was my very first kidnapping. Next time I'll know how to react.'

'You have not got out of this one yet,' he reminded her, looking down at her in the dim light.

'It's only a matter of time. Now even more people know where I am. You can't just—just hang on to me.'

'The inclination is there. Why do you think I have kept you out here now?'

'I assumed I had broken some obscure rule.' She glared at him, but he gave an unexpected laugh and pulled her towards him.

'Not that I can think of,' he murmured, staring into her eyes. 'It seemed like a good time to have you to myself for a moment.'

'There's absolutely no need,' April pointed out breathlessly. 'Everyone believes your story except Petros. We don't have to act it out any more.'

'Perhaps I need to. The more I touch you, the more I want to. I can't keep my hands off you.'

She was locked in his arms before she could move, and there was no longer any laughter in his voice. He pulled her into the shadows, leaning against the wall and holding her tightly against him.

'The—the servants will come for the cups,' she gasped, frantically turning her head away from his searching lips. 'Your mother will come and . . .'

Nothing could stop him and April gave a sigh that was almost contentment as his lips found hers and covered them urgently. When he tightened her to him even more she simply collapsed against him. It was warm, heaven. When Michalis held her, nothing stayed in her mind at all. She could not remember one thing to tell herself that would make her draw back. Her arms went round his neck and he began to caress her fiercely, running his hands over her back, her waist and the slender length of her arms.

His teeth caught her lower lip urgently and then moved to tug erotically at her earlobe and when his hand slid to her breast she cried out with delight, a little whimpering sound of excitement that he heard only too well.

'You feel like this with Petros?' he asked against her ear, his breath ragged in his throat. 'Do you catch fire and melt into him? Does he hear those strange little cries of delight when he touches you?'

'No,' she moaned and his hand slid into the neck of her dress, searching for the silken warmth of her breast, closing round it as it surged to fill his hand.

'No,' he agreed unevenly. 'He did not pull you into his arms that night in your room, he clasped your knees like a grateful boy and hugged you. Perhaps I came before you had time to pat his head. It is, I think, all he would have got. I was wildly angry, but not too angry to see that your body was not making the signals to him that it makes to me.' His fingers teased her nipple, bringing it to even more excitement, and his mouth opened over hers as she cried out feverishly. 'Be grateful that we are not alone,' he breathed against her mouth. 'If we were, tonight I would take you, whatever you are, whoever you are.'

When she was almost sobbing in his arms, he straightened up and put her away from him, smoothing her hair and then looking down at her in the near-darkness. She could only look back helplessly and his smile was back to being sardonic, even though his eyes glittered with fire.

'Yes,' he said derisively. 'You are two people—a mind and a body. The mind is evasive and devious, but the body is mine.'

He turned and walked into the house, and April stood for a few minutes in the cool night air, trying to recover and not succeeding very well. When she managed to pluck up the necessary courage to go indoors he was waiting for her, leaning against the door that led to the *sala*.

'You wish to plead a bad head and escape to your room?' he enquired in amusement. It somewhat restored April's wandering senses and she managed a pretty ferocious glare.

'I do not! I can face them if you can. After all, you're carrying a greater burden of guilt. I'm a guest here. If you want to shock your mother, just keep on as you are because soon she'll find out this is all a lie.'

'Which particular lie are we speaking of?' he enquired quizzically. 'She merely thinks that you are my girlfriend. She is very happy about that. Are you about to tell her that you are also the passionate friend of Petros? It is a little too late, *pethi*. She has seen you with me, locked in my arms and very willing to be there, delighting in my caresses. I do not think she would believe you.'

'I don't care!' April snapped. 'Sooner or later I'll be away from here.'

'At the moment I think it will be later,' he threatened softly. 'Perhaps much later. I must get you a postcard to send to your mother. I will help you to write it.'

Of course he was merely taunting, but there was a look in his eyes that was unfathomable and April felt a thrill that was not altogether alarm. She was grateful when Marika suddenly appeared and grabbed her arm.

'There you are,' she said firmly. 'Let us talk about dresses. Michalis keeps you to himself all the time. I have some good ideas about tomorrow.'

April glanced at Michalis and found to her anxiety that those carved lips were twisted in a smile of malicious amusement. He was not beaten. There was something he knew and she was not at all sure what it was. He looked like someone who had the upper hand, and as that was quite normal with him it gave her great qualms.

CHAPTER NINE

NEXT day, Michalis seemed to be doing everything possible to keep his family on edge. In the first place, the helicopter did not arrive at ten and he showed no sign of annoyance at that. He was more easygoing than April had ever seen, and her anxiety at the delay was matched by that of Petros.

'I have seen him when orders have been disobeyed,' he muttered to April. 'Normally we would have thunderous looks and the telephone line to Athens would be almost on fire. He's taking this too calmly; therefore, he planned it.'

'What advantage would it give him?' April wanted to know. This was the last day and Michalis would not have had to do anything at all to make her uneasy—she was uneasy enough without help.

'I do not know,' Petros said worriedly. 'I think it is too late to pull out of this betrothal, but then again it is Michalis. He is a law unto himself. Who knows what he has found out? He may seem to have been here, taking a short rest with his family, but I know that brain. It never stops; neither do his assistants. At any time, day or night, they know they can ring him if anything happens that would interest him.'

Marika was edgy for quite another reason.

'It will delay things,' she grumbled. 'What about the shopping for April?'

'There is the day after this,' Michalis said unconcernedly when she tackled him. It gave April a thrill and

154

an anxiety. He was not letting her go. Her eyes met his but he did not smile, not even in his sardonic manner. He was giving nothing away and she was left biting her lip, worrying and trying to guess what he had in mind. It was an impossibility. Even Petros was mystified and unsettled.

The first party did not leave until just before lunch, and afterwards April went to her room to pack. Michalis had seen them off and had spoken to the pilot but he had not looked as if he was handing out any reprimands. Now she was left with just the four of them, and the house seemed decidedly empty. It also seemed to be filled with menace.

It was well into the afternoon before Petros left with Marika, and April had to endure the parting with a bright smile. She would not see either of them again, and impulsively she hugged Marika close. She had taken a great liking to the girl and it was something of a wrench to see her go, especially as Marika was excitedly planning their shopping trip right to the end, even calling out as she was firmly shut in for take-off.

'Now there are just the two of us,' Michalis pointed out as the silver machine rose into the air. 'We are back where we started.'

'How long will it be?' April asked uneasily as she watched the helicopter out of sight, but all she got was a careless shrug.

'Who knows?' It made her stop and look at him suspiciously. It was not the sort of remark he made, and such inefficiency would never be tolerated.

'What are you going to do?' She looked very anxious and this brought a sardonic smile to his face.

'I am going to wait, naturally. Or do you mean what am I going to do with you? Perhaps I have not decided.'

When she wanted to ask more he simply looked at her darkly and walked away. He was going into his study and she felt unable to follow him there. Even if she listened at the door she would not be able to understand any telephone calls and there was always the possibility of being discovered by a servant. There was nothing to do but wait.

She was still waiting as the sky grew dark. She was dressed for travel in her navy blue dress, and although she might look demure she felt nothing like that inside. Michalis was doing what he had been doing all day—making the tension rise—and she could no longer hope that this was either a mistake or inefficiency. The chance of getting a plane tonight was remote to say the least.

April refused to beg. Dinner was served and she managed to contain her anxiety until almost the end. It finally got the better of her. Michalis just wasn't speaking at all. The house was silent except for the few discreet servants and she was almost ready to scream.

'When is the helicopter coming back?' she suddenly burst out.

'It is not.' He sat back in his seat and looked at her levelly, no expression on his face.

'How do you know? Have you heard something?'

'I have heard nothing at all. It is not coming back because I told the pilot not to bring it. He will arrive when I call him.'

'What about my plane?' April just stared at him wildly and he picked up his glass, taking a sip of wine and looking at her with irritating calm.

'Your plane? You are not booked on to a flight. As far as I can tell you have plenty of time. There is the matter of the postcard, but that can be dealt with.'

'You have to be at this betrothal ceremony,' she pointed out, but he shrugged again and went on watching her.

'It is to take place tomorrow instead. I had a word with Kyrios Martis and my mother. They were in agreement. It will give Madame Martis more time to recover and from their house we can go directly to my boat. It is better. It will make the joyous occasion last longer, well into the night. I have arranged for fireworks.'

'What does Petros think?'

'He agrees. I had a private word with him.' He sat looking at her steadily and she found herself trembling. Had he told Petros that the game was up? Had he sent them off only to cancel it later?

'Are they engaged?' she asked anxiously, her eyes wide on his handsome face.

'They are. You know that perfectly well. It was arranged this afternoon. Kyrios Martis and I could have done it alone after all—we are both heads of our respective families. The rest is merely celebration, and of course Stella's mother must be included before we have our big celebration on the boat.'

'Petros never told me that,' she remarked shakily.

'Perhaps he did not want a scene when you realised it was final. In any case,' he added quietly, 'I noted that my brother was filled with anxiety. That is why I had a private word with him too. We would not want the Martis family to think that he regretted this venture, would we?'

April knew he was toying with her, taunting, even though his face was perfectly serious.

'What about me?' she whispered.

'But you are with me, April. You have always been with me. You will come to the celebrations. First we will get you a beautiful gown and then you will join my family.'

She jumped up, agitated and wary, staring at him wildly, ready to run.

'What cruelty are you planning now? Let me go home! What do you want to keep me here for? It's all over. Petros is engaged and the family honour is secure. There's nothing left to do.'

He stood slowly and faced her, the length of the table between them.

'Is there not?' he asked softly. 'I think there is. Once again we are alone, *despinis*, but by now I think you are very much attached to your captor. I want to find out how much.' He began to walk towards her but April knew what those arms could do to her, how he could pull her into the spell. She turned and ran, not stopping when he called, ignoring his quiet laughter, and she was almost at the door of her room when he caught her.

'Get out!' She tried to close the door but his hand was there, flat and uncompromising, holding the door open with very little effort. She was getting more distressed by the minute and for a second she didn't even hear his quiet words.

'April. He has told me.' She just went on struggling and he used more force, just enough to make her give up and back away.

'April,' he said softly. 'Have you been listening to me? Petros has told me everything.'

'He can't have, because it would ruin his life. When you know about the Martis family you'll stop the engagement.'

'I'll *what*?' He stood quite still and looked at her rather desperate face. 'What about the Martis family?' April turned away, biting at her lip. She had just blurted it out and now he would probe until he found out more.

'Nothing,' she said lamely.

'Just because you look like a young girl there is no need to behave like one,' he pointed out drily, grasping her shoulder and spinning her to face him. 'I have told you they are betrothed. It is settled. Even if I were inclined to do so I would not be able to change things, and if you recall I have been most anxious to see that they got on with matters speedily.'

'You—you can't change things?' she asked anxiously.

'I cannot and I do not wish to. Now what is this about Stella's family?' When she did not answer and avoided his eyes he gave a low, dark laugh. 'Could you be talking about their financial problems, I wonder?'

'So you did know after all?'

'How could I not? My dear Miss Stewart, I have a finger on the pulse of the business world. Very little occurs that does not filter down to me very quickly. I have known for some time. That is what the meeting was about when I took you to Athens with me. We were trying to come up with a plan to rescue Stella's father. The plan was easy; getting him to accept help was a little more difficult. He is a proud man and kept quiet about it. None of us cared to approach him immediately. Fortunately he decided to tell me himself when he came here yesterday. You heard him ask to speak to me, surely?'

'He decided to risk that?' April asked in awe.

'He is a man of honour. In any case, what risk?' Michalis was looking at her as if she were amusingly mad.

'Well, surely he was scared that you might cancel the betrothal if you knew they were poor?'

He looked at her in amazement for a second, his black brows raised, and then his eyes narrowed with understanding.

'So this is why I am a—what was your expression?— a money-grabbing toad?'

'Petros and Stella thought you would refuse to let them become engaged if you found out and—and that was why he...' April blushed wildly and looked away.

'And that was why he needed your help in his little drama,' Michalis finished grimly. 'His confession did not go quite that far. He merely told me that you were not at all to blame, that you had been unaware of his plans until you came to the island.'

'Why didn't he tell me things were all right before he left?' She could still not really believe that everything was cleared up, out in the open. But most of all she could not believe that Michalis had taken this so calmly. Why wasn't he angry?

'He did not tell you because I asked him not to. He owed me that much, don't you think?'

'So that's why you let them all go and kept me here?' April asked shakily. 'I knew you'd be furious when you found out. Now you're going to punish me, aren't you?'

'It is one way of looking at it,' he agreed. 'You have caused me a great deal of trouble, accused me of being more interested in money than the happiness of my brother. You have joined in a deliberate lie. Surely you deserve punishment?'

She didn't know what he was intending but he had a look about him that showed her he thought it perfectly all right to discipline her. It brought April to her senses and her temper rose rapidly. She had no idea how she had come to want this arrogant man but she was not about to submit to harsh treatment like a slave.

'If you think I'm going to stand here and let you chastise me you can think again,' she snapped, turning to glare at him. 'You seem to have forgotten who really suffered in this. *I* was kidnapped, and you're not getting away with it!'

'There is really nothing you can do, *pethi*. I have not let you go,' he said softly, moving towards her like a panther.

'I can scream the house down!' she threatened.

'And you know what I will do. Still, it is what you want, is it not? You want my arms around you.'

'I don't!' Once again he had worked April up into a turmoil and she felt tears of angry frustration filling her eyes. He was keeping her here to torment her, to pay her back for helping Petros. He was so sure of his power, so ruthless that he just crushed ordinary people—her most of all. 'I hate you!' she cried.

She raised her hands to attack him, wildly hurt and miserable, but her wrists were caught in an iron grip as he held her in front of him, looking down into her tear-filled eyes. April struggled but he held her wrists tightly until she just let the tears fall and bowed her head in defeat.

Michalis said nothing but his hands relaxed their hold and moved to cup her face. When she raised her head he was looking at her seriously and he stroked back her hair and began to kiss the tears away with such gentleness that she could only look at him in wonder. When his hands moved to stroke her neck, her cheeks and her eyes she felt every part of her relax from tension, and still he said nothing at all.

They just stood there with their eyes locked together and April found herself drowning in the glittering darkness, hypnotised again, falling into the velvet abyss.

He reached across to close the door, his eyes never leaving hers, and she never protested when his fingers began to unbutton her dress. It slid to her waist and her tiny lace bra seemed to drift away at the gentle persuasion of his hands.

When he looked down at her she felt her breasts swell, and he touched them almost tenderly before looking back into her eyes. And it was just as hypnotic to her when he unfastened his own shirt and let it fall to the floor before drawing her trembling hands to his chest. She found her fingers searching the hard muscles, clenching in the light covering of crisp dark hair, and then he took her hand in his, leading her to the bed.

'Come, *karithia*,' he said softly.

He let her dress slide to the floor and then gently pushed her down and stood looking at her. April stared at him with bewitched eyes, and he knelt beside the bed, stroking away her last garment with caressing hands that began to explore her body with a magical touch that brought whimpers of delight to her lips. He leaned over her, kissing every part of her with delicate kisses that made her senses swim, bringing her to such a level of sensitivity that she began to moan softly in her throat, unable to keep still.

When he came at last to join her on the bed, his own clothes discarded, she knew how vulnerable he had made her, how fragile against such power, and belatedly she remembered his words at the house on the cliff. He had promised nothing but to be what he was—a fierce male animal who desired her. She was aching with passion and when she looked up into the face that hovered over her she saw a raw need that made her limbs tense from their delighted lethargy.

'Michalis!' His name would scarcely leave her lips but he had felt her fear, recognised the swift change to tense waiting at the taut pressure of his body.

'No fears, no bitterness,' he said huskily, 'just you and me where we belong, where we would have been days ago if others had not entered our lives.' He stroked back her hair, his fingers tracing her eyebrows and then the delicate curve of her ears. He bent his head, lightly kissing her breasts, catching her to him when she called out in bewilderment as shafts of pleasure tore through her. 'If we had only just met it would have made little difference,' he murmured against her lips. 'Very quickly you would have been in my arms. No fear, *karithia*.'

He began to caress her again, holding her close, delighting her all over again until the powerful body held no fears and the relentless pressure to possess her became what she wanted too, her wild little moans telling him. His lips covered her last wild cry as he entered her and then the dark force was all around her and inside her, masterful, intense, controlling her fall as she slid at last into the black velvet chasm that seemed to have been calling her since she first looked into his eyes.

It was like being in a sweetly violent storm, tossed in the waves of hunger that lapped at her soul until brilliant stars beckoned and she soared up into the sky, clinging to the wonderful heat that had enveloped her.

April did not know she was calling his name over and over in gasping breaths until he cupped her face and gently covered her mouth with his. When he raised his head and looked down at her she gazed back in bewilderment and then began to cry helplessly, hot, heavy tears that fell like rain unchecked down her flushed cheeks. The relief of days of tension had left her utterly vul-

nerable, and Michalis just held her, making no attempt
to stop her at all.

When she finally buried herself against his shoulder,
choking back the sobs, he lifted her face and wiped her
wet cheeks, and she blinked up at him, biting her lips
together.

'Is—is it always like that?' she whispered.

He looked into the tear-wet sparkling grey of her eyes
and shook his head. 'I think not. I have never felt like
that—never felt such hunger, never been utterly without
control, at the mercy of my feelings. No woman has given
herself to me so completely that she finally wept in my
arms.'

April tried to turn away, flushing even more at his
words, but he turned her back to him, his gaze running
over her face like a caress.

'You were perfect,' he said thickly. 'For a moment I
thought we would die together.' She smiled up at him,
reassured that he had felt the same overwhelming magic,
but his face was serious and he touched her cheek almost
reverently. 'I would not have minded,' he finished quietly.

April's smile died too and she looked up into his eyes
until he groaned softly and covered her mouth with his
again in a deep, yearning kiss that never seemed to end.
Her arms moved around his neck, clinging tightly to him.
For the moment she had no thought in her head, no
feelings in her heart but for Michalis. She seemed to have
given her whole mind and body to him, even her soul.

When at last she lay beside him, enclosed in his arms,
she was too filled with emotion to speak, and his hands
stroked her as if he could do nothing else.

'You wish to leave me?' he asked deeply. 'You want
an end to your captivity?' She could only shake her head.
It was not possible to think, to plan, to remember any

other life. He seemed to relax and he drew her closer. 'Then you belong to me?'

'Yes,' April whispered. Even as she said it she compared her life with his. She knew how wealthy he was, how important. The woman in his life would have to be sophisticated, glittering, important herself, a carefully chosen partner who could match his lifestyle, have his children—an heiress from such another important family. And Greek. She would have to be Greek.

'What are you thinking?' he probed quietly. 'You are silent but that energetic little mind is busy. I can feel it.'

'I was thinking about your life,' April confessed, 'your importance.'

He gave an irritated grunt and moved just far enough to look at her. 'You mean my hard work, my daily duties, my responsibilities? I have many possessions, a great deal of wealth, but inside I am like anyone else.'

'Weak, vulnerable and defenceless?' April asked in amusement, pulling herself up to look down at him sceptically. He grinned and nipped at her skin and then enclosed her in hard arms.

'Only when I want you,' he said softly. 'Be still and go to sleep. I am tired. I have used up all my emotion and it is a dangerous state to be in. If I get any messages tonight I will be quite uninterested.'

'Do they even phone to your bedroom?' April asked in awe.

'Yes. Quite frequently.'

'But you're in my room,' she pointed out, and he tightened her to him, settling them more comfortably.

'Then they will not find me,' he assured her sleepily. 'I am hiding with you. Go to sleep, my beautiful little wretch. I have not had a good night's sleep since I first met you.'

April snuggled into his arms, pushing her fears and doubts away. Tomorrow she would face them. If he wanted her to stay she would stay because she knew that whatever happened she would never be able simply to go away and forget Michalis. Since they had met there had been intense feelings—fear, anger and then this burning desire, and for her . . . love; she knew it now.

She tried to think of the future but then pushed it out of her mind because she could not see any future. There was this yawning chasm that would not be bridged by desire, and after a while Michalis would turn away from her and go back to his own kind of people.

When she awoke next day it was already sunny and hot, the morning well advanced, and she looked round in embarrassment as a maid came in with her breakfast. Michalis was gone but it seemed to her that anyone would know he had been here. To her overwrought senses he seemed to be still in the room. But the maid simply smiled and placed the tray on her lap.

'Kyrios Konstantine said you would have breakfast in your room,' she said. 'We were not sure what to give you, but he told us fruit juice, tea and we have made toast. It is good, *despinis*?'

'It's very good, thank you,' April assured her with a flushed face. 'Kyrios Konstantine made a good guess.' The maid's eyes seemed to be twinkling with satisfaction and April wondered if the servants too were anxious to see him married. She went to have a wash and then came back to climb into bed and eat her breakfast. The lap of luxury! She smiled to herself, remembering her own little flat. How different she was from Michalis. The thought made her almost mournful and he walked in while she still had the saddened expression on her face.

'The breakfast is not good?' he enquired as she looked up at him almost miserably.

'It—it's fine. Should you be here? I mean, should you just walk in when a maid might come up and...?'

'I have been here all night,' he reminded her softly. 'Wherever we are tonight, I will be right beside you. I have little time for pretending. Is that why you seem so unhappy?'

'No. I was thinking about my flat. I was remembering how small it is. It seems a long time since I was there.'

Michalis removed the tray and sat beside her, lifting her into his arms and looking into her eyes.

'Do you regret last night?' he asked tensely. 'Do you wish it had never happened?'

'Oh, no! I—I was just thinking, that's all.'

'Are you going to leave me, April?' He cupped her face fiercely and stared into her eyes, everything about him taut and waiting.

'Well, I'll have to go back—eventually.' She wanted him to say he loved her, but he never said anything and she found herself almost babbling. 'I have responsibilities too, you know. I have a house to do this month and then there's my flat and—and I've got things...like a teddy-bear I've had for years...'

Michalis began to smile, a slow, long smile that grew across his face, touched his dark eyes and banished his tension.

'How can just one woman do all this to me?' he asked softly. 'How can she infuriate me, puzzle me, entrance and delight me? How can a wild, furious girl with a flashing temper, who risked her life to escape me, lie quietly in my arms and worry about a teddy-bear? I will have it collected and flown out here.'

'Am I staying?' April asked, looking up at him wistfully.

'To leave me, you would have to escape.' He looked serious again and held her closer. 'Don't ask me to let you go, not while I am still bewitched by last night.'

'I'm—I'm your mistress?' she asked in a trembling voice, and for a minute he looked down at her seriously before she saw the smile grow again, this time with a wicked twinkle at the back of dark eyes.

'Yes,' he said positively. 'I think I like the sound of that. You are my mistress. You will like that, *karithia*? You will be pleased when I tell *Mitera*, when I introduce you tonight to my friends who will join us on the boat? What shall I say? This is April, my mistress. She is English. Will that be good?'

'I—I don't know...' Her voice trailed away and he caught her close, kissing her urgently, his hands twisted in her hair.

'You are doing it again,' he breathed. 'You are surprising me, enchanting me. I want to make love to you and there is no time.' He lifted her away and stood looking down at her, his cheekbones flushed with desire. 'Eat your breakfast quickly,' he said huskily. 'The helicopter is already on its way. I have a lot of things to do today and for some of the time I will have to leave you with *Mitera*, but first I will buy you the gown for tonight. Marika shall not have that pleasure. I want you to myself.'

He went out, leaving her bemused, and she was suddenly too excited to eat; she had to force any food down. He only had to be there and she didn't care at all about the future. She loved him so much that whatever he said she knew she would follow like a slave.

* * *

When they arrived in Athens his car was waiting. There were other cars too and as far as she could see there were at least three secretaries and a couple of men who looked extremely important and not a little restless. They all wanted to speak to Michalis and however impatient he looked he had to read papers that were pushed at him, give quick orders and arrange meetings. He could never escape from his empire, it followed him around, and April felt like an outsider, an alien, almost a country bumpkin with limited intelligence.

'At last!' He gave low growl of irritation as he got into the car and drove away. 'The time has come when Petros must take some of this weight from me. When he is married he will earn his keep. I have no time for myself any more.'

April sat by him a little anxiously because he was suddenly the Michalis she had first met, the powerful, dark being who had looked down at her like a god. She could hardly believe that last night he had been tender, had filled her with passion that even now was making her feel lethargic and complete.

'Do not be so anxious,' he suddenly said, glancing across at her. 'I am not about to make you work; after all, you are my mistress, as we have agreed. I shall keep you in luxury.' He was smiling to himself but it made April's cheeks red and it did nothing for her self-confidence.

'Michalis——' she began worriedly, but his hand closed over hers and he lifted it to his lips.

'Hush, *karithia*,' he said softly. 'You belong to me. There is nothing at all to fear. Just wait until tonight when you are the most beautiful woman on my boat.'

Announced as his mistress so that everyone could envy her and look at her as if she was to be secretly despised.

April bit her soft lip and kept silent but her heart was hammering with anxiety and she dreaded being out of his sight.

She had no idea where they were going. The day was now very hot, the traffic horrendous, but they eventually came to calmer streets and April's heart took off to a crescendo as she recognised the quiet, rich suburb where she had been imprisoned before, the house with white shutters that stood by the little park.

Michalis drew up outside and turned to look at her.

'Wait here,' he said quietly. 'I have an announcement to make that is secret even from you. The lady inside will not be expecting it and she may need a few moments to recover from the surprise. I will not be long and then we will go to the shops.'

He got out, and she watched him stride across the road, her brain still reeling. His mistress lived here; he had admitted it. Now he was going to tell her that he had someone else. He had also said that this woman had wealth of her own. He was discarding her readily and April had a picture of her own future. He would tire of her too and send her away, back to England. Would he give her time to recover as he was giving this woman time? Would he send her away gently? Would she have to live through the misery and the torment of seeing him turn to someone else?

She got out of the car, clutching her bag, standing in the hot street. People were looking at her curiously but she never even saw them. Suddenly she was frantic. In this short time she had grown to love Michalis until she could think of nothing else. How would she be after a few years? It might only be a few months, or weeks. She looked round like a trapped animal and when a taxi passed close by she came to life, raising her arm and running into the road.

'Taxi!' As he stopped she almost fell on the door, worried that he would not speak English. 'The airport!' She was almost shouting, relief making her legs weak when he nodded and leaned back to open the door for her.

'Yes, *despinis*. Right away.'

She sank back into the seat, knowing she had left her luggage behind. She had left happiness behind too. Michalis would recover quickly. She wasn't sure if she would ever recover but she would not be waiting each day to be discarded like the woman in that house. She would have her dignity, her flat, her job and her mother. If she stayed with Michalis she would finally have nothing but a broken heart.

CHAPTER TEN

APRIL knew that Michalis would come after her. At this moment he wanted her and he would not gladly let her escape. The chance of a flight was slim indeed but she had to try. Perhaps he would not think she had come here, not with her luggage in his car and left behind. She pushed her way forward at the airport and put her return half of the ticket down on the counter. The whole ticket had been open-ended, to use as she pleased, and she wanted to use it now almost frantically.

'Can you get me on to a flight to London?' she asked breathlessly.

'At short notice? I doubt it, *despinis*.'

'It's an emergency,' April babbled, and after glancing at her desperate face the woman at the desk decided that it probably was. She checked her list and then looked up at the flight board.

'There is a flight almost ready to leave and there is just one seat, a cancellation, but you may not want that seat.'

'I do! I do!' April was almost at the stage of looking over her shoulder, and any seat would be welcome, even if she had to sit on the captain's knee.

'It is in the smoking section,' the woman announced seriously. 'They will be smoking.'

'I don't care if they're having a bath,' April muttered, pushing her ticket forward. 'Get me on it.'

She was on it very speedily, rushed on at the last minute and hurried to her seat as the door was closed. She didn't feel safe until the plane began to move, so sure of the power that Michalis wielded that she felt he could order it to stop and recapture her. She only rested back as the plane became airborne and then it was time for secret tears, for deep, agonised longing and for facing a future without Michalis.

She never saw the Mercedes tear up to the airport as the plane took off, and if she had she would not have understood. Michalis got out but his wild drive had not been successful and he knew it. He looked up at the sky, watching the plane climb higher and higher.

'Go in!' Marika urged almost violently, shaking his sleeve.

'Yes, I will go in,' he agreed, his eyes on the plane, 'but it will be too late. She is up there. I will watch her go.'

'How do you even know that the plane is the one for England? How do you know that April is on it? You cannot know!'

'I know,' he said softly, and when Marika turned to look at him in agitation he was smiling to himself, a curious smile that had her baffled. 'I know, little sister,' he assured her, patting her hand. 'I also know why.'

April contemplated her flat gloomily. She had once been delighted with it, proud of her own innovations, but now it looked lifeless, lonely, probably because that was how she felt herself. In truth, she had not been here much since she returned to England almost three weeks ago. She had been at home, getting to know her new family, grateful for their affection.

Nothing had turned out as she had imagined. She had gone there expecting trouble, more hurt, but they had been waiting for her impatiently, a united family eager to claim her back.

'You're a very special girl, April,' Edwin Burton told her quietly, smiling into her eyes. 'Your mother can be proud of you. We're all proud of you. This house was such a surprise to us when we came back.'

With her mother in grateful tears and Edwin looking dangerously close to them himself, April couldn't find anything to say. Her mother would not be proud if she knew everything. She could hardly tell them. It would mean bringing Gail into the conversation, and so far Gail had not even appeared.

She had appeared then, looking shy and worried, smiling at April and clearly not expecting a smile in return.

'Thank you for my room,' she managed anxiously. 'I know you spent a lot of time on it, and a lot of money. I saw those curtains and the duvet cover when I was out with my mother, but she said they were too expensive. It looks so lovely, April, and you did it for me.'

'To make you feel at home,' April pointed out. 'This is your home now. I've got my own place.'

'I know I've been awful and I don't deserve any favours, but can't you move back in here, April?' Gail asked wistfully. 'I've never had a sister before.'

They were smiling and hugging each other in minutes, and from then on, if April was not at home, Gail found some excuse to come to the flat almost daily, cycling round on her way from school until April felt that she had known the girl for years. It was some consolation for all her pain and misery. She had made someone happy and her plan had worked.

It was a week before she told her mother the truth. The questions about her holiday were getting too difficult to answer. The tears always threatened, and one night when she was sitting with her mother and new stepfather she burst into tears and the truth came pouring out.

There were no recriminations. Her mother held her close and Edwin had rage on his face, the first time she had ever seen him angry. They knew nothing about why she had finally escaped. They did not know that she and Michalis had become lovers, even though for a brief time. That heartache she kept to herself.

Now the days were long, warm and sunny but they seemed drear to April. There were no jobs either. Her last commission was almost finished and there was nothing at all lined up after it. The wolf was finally at the door and April had spent the morning contemplating her future with the aid of the local paper and the ads for employment. Nobody wanted an art-school-trained interior designer, with or without experience.

Her money was almost gone and action would have to be taken. In the first place, her car would have to go, then, perhaps, this flat. Well, she could always go back home. At least that was secure. She was gloomily staring at the wall, finishing her lunch, when the bell rang and she sprang up to answer without much thought, thinking it was Gail—and stopped in surprise to look warily at the man who stood outside.

He was well dressed and very smooth-looking, middle-aged and definitely prosperous, but there was something about him that had her standing on the defensive, the door in her hand ready to be slammed.

'Miss Stewart? Miss April Stewart, the interior designer?'

April had never been called *the* interior designer before and it rather stunned her.

'Yes.' She bit back the inclination to apologise for lack of grandeur, and he smiled pleasantly.

'Very good! I do hope you're free this afternoon? My name is Willis. I'm a housing agent.'

'Don't you mean estate agent?' April asked suspiciously, her eyes still wary.

'No, Miss Stewart—housing agent. We have a commission for you—a good deal of work.'

'It's usual to phone,' April said sternly, but she got the same little smile.

'This is urgent. In fact, it is so urgent that we were hoping you could pop along and see it right now.'

It was a time for fast thinking. She wasn't at all easy in her mind about this man, but business was not exactly booming at the moment and a country house was not to be dismissed readily.

'Normally,' she pointed out in a brisk manner, 'the—er—lady of the house contacts me.'

'They're away overseas, and they wanted the place done before they get back. You'll have a free hand of course, no expense spared.'

It was a very big and very juicy carrot, and April bit her lip thoughtfully. Normally Gail would be here. It was half-term and April had been expecting her all morning. She didn't like going off when nobody knew where she was; her days of adventure were over. Even so, she couldn't let this pass.

'All right,' she said uneasily. 'I can come immediately, providing it's not too far.'

'A few miles. I have my car outside.'

'I have mine,' April informed him stiffly. 'If you'll get into your car, I'll get my bag and follow you.' Now she really *was* suspicious but, weighing everything up, she couldn't see much harm if she kept her wits about her, and it might just be genuine.

The car was genuine all right—a red Porsche that didn't exactly suit the character of the man who was driving it but which proved some sort of money. He got in when he saw her, that odd smile still intact, and April stopped to look down at him forbiddingly.

'Pull out and I'll be right behind you,' she said, frowning at him. 'I'm driving a very infirm Ford. Keep your speed down.'

She got a cheerful nod and they were soon leaving the town behind and heading for the country. She was not at all happy about this; only the threat of poverty forced her forward. Every defensive instinct seemed to be leaping about inside her, and when he finally pulled into a lane she wound up every window and locked every door. It might be an old Ford but it would take more muscle than he had to get her out of it.

The lane went on for quite a while, and just when she was thinking of reversing back to the main road and forgetting the whole matter he turned in at a gate and drove down a drive between high hedges. It was all very, very secluded, and April was sharply on guard.

The drive ended in front of a medium-sized white Georgian house, and as the Porsche swung round the circular, gravelled end of the drive April braked and stared at the house bleakly. She could probably forget the job. This looked like Spooky Hollow to her. Shout for help here and you wouldn't be heard for miles.

There wasn't even any traffic sound. There were squirrels dashing about the lawn like so many tame cats, and for all she knew this was a deserted place, empty and abandoned in spite of the gloss of the outside. She

sat right where she was and looked through the wind-
screen grimly.

Mr Willis came walking over to her and now he was
beaming, as if he had achieved some secret goal. It confirmed her suspicions and she fixed him with clear grey
eyes, determined to be dominant.

'I'll just show you round,' he said cheerfully, bending
to look in at her and dangling a large set of keys in his
hand like bait. April wound the window down just
enough to be able to speak clearly, ready to bite him if
he so much as looked eager.

'I'll show myself around, Mr Willis,' she said briefly,
'when you've gone.'

'I'm supposed to let you in.'

'We'll pretend that you did,' April promised drily.
'Just tell me where to leave the keys after I've finished
and I'm sure you can drive off. You're probably busy.'

'If you imagine for one moment——' he began huffily,
but April didn't even let him finish.

'Look! I've seen this play before; in fact, I had a
leading role. You don't depart—I drive off.'

For a moment he looked annoyed enough to tell her
he would get someone else, but he pulled himself together
and managed a rather wintry smile.

'I suppose you're wise to be cautious, but there is no
need. I'll go back to town. Sure you can find your way
back?'

'Perfectly certain,' April assured him, taking the keys
and quickly winding the window back up. If he thought
she was mad it was his problem. She wasn't setting one
foot outside until that Porsche went.

He drove away and she watched him intently, her eyes
on the rear-view mirror, and then she gave him an extra
few minutes just in case. When she got out she stood

very still, listening carefully, and not until she could hear nothing but birdsong did she move away from the car. There had been a time when she would have cheerfully come here as innocently and eagerly as a child. Not any more.

It reminded her how safe she had felt with Michalis, even when he had captured her. It had only been that first burst of fear, and after that there had been safety even though she had tried to escape from it. Now she saw danger in everything, and mostly it was because part of her was missing—a part of her mind was always back in Greece, back with Michalis.

She let herself into the house and carefully locked the door behind her. Even so, she was taking a risk and she knew it. He could come back, but she had been very cautious, and if this really was a commission it was a good one—too good to turn down because of fright.

When she turned away from locking the door she stood quite still with a puzzled frown on her face. It wasn't the deserted house she had imagined. There was a well-kept air about it, and at first glance she would have said that the last thing it needed was renovation. There were some very good pictures in the hall and a white fringed Indian carpet that looked very expensive. If the rest of the house was like this then she was altering nothing at all without specific instructions.

Double doors led into another room and when she opened them she found herself in a beautiful drawing-room, again perfect to her experienced eye, and April's frown deepened as odd shivers began to run down her spine. Now she really doubted if there had been any commission at all, and fear began to grow inside with every move she made. It wasn't just because she longed for Michalis. It wasn't just that part of her mind was far away. This was dangerous. She had to get out of here—fast!

When she spun round to head for the hall again, she stopped dead. Neatly arranged by the wall, just behind the door, was a suitcase. Beside it sat two smaller ones. They were closed, the travel labels still on them, and she did not have to read the labels. The suitcases were hers and the last time she had seen them was in Greece, in Athens, and in the car Michalis had been driving. Her face went pale and she gripped the settee with shaking hands. Someone had brought them and she dared not to think who.

She was still standing there, trembling and weak, when Michalis stepped into the hall from another room and came slowly towards her.

'You are very careless about your possessions, *pethi*,' he said softly, standing still in the doorway and watching her with dark, intent eyes. 'I think in future it would be best if you left all the luggage to me.'

April couldn't speak. Her heart was hammering as if it wanted to leap from her chest. Her eyes were wide open, dazzlingly grey and clear with lingering fear still at the back of them.

Michalis went to a cabinet and poured himself a drink as she watched in disbelief, and she turned slowly to follow him with her eyes as he walked across and sat down in a large chair by the fireplace.

'I observed that you finally managed your escape,' he said quietly, and she almost collapsed on the settee, her eyes locked with his.

'What—what are you doing here in this house?' she asked.

'The company owns it. We own quite a lot of property and this is newly acquired. It is private and convenient, quite close to your home.'

'You don't know where I live,' April assured him without much hope.

'I know you have a flat and I know the address. Petros wrote to you there, my mother sent your ticket there. I know your own mother lives close by. What else is there to know?'

'That—that man...Mr Willis. He works for you. It was a trick.'

'Of course it was a trick. I watched your precautions from the window. I approve. You have become much more careful.'

'You lied to get me here!' April looked at him accusingly and he nodded with every appearance of satisfaction.

'I am getting the hang of it.'

The laconic reply brought April to her feet and she glared at him bitterly. 'What a waste of time. Thank you for bringing my luggage and now, if you don't mind, I'll go.'

When she turned to leave he was instantly on his feet, taking her arm and holding her still. It drove her wild. She wanted to just turn and look at him, tell him that she had missed him every second of every day, but he was still the same, still only wanting a mistress, and his determined tracking of her only showed how ruthless he could be.

'I do mind. I have come for you, April. I want you with me, back in Greece.'

'Until you decide to get another mistress? Until you tell me the way you told that woman in Athens? Do you think I'm just going to go on being a captive?'

'I hope so,' he said quietly, turning her to face him and noticing the way her eyes were glazed with tears. 'I hope it will be the longest captivity in the world.'

'The woman—I—can't...'

'The woman in the house in Athens was my mother,' he said softly. 'I told you it was my house but in fact it is only that on paper. My mother lives there for much of the time. She likes the city life.'

April just stood and looked at him. She could not believe it. She wanted to believe it but such things did not happen—not to her.

'Why did you run, *karithia*?' he asked deeply, and she turned away again, struggling with tears.

'You said you wanted to tell that woman who lived there. I thought... You were going to take me to the boat and introduce me as your mistress. I couldn't do that.'

'Why, April? You knew how I felt about you.'

'I knew you wanted me, for the time being. I knew they would imagine that I—I just wanted your money, the glamour, just another woman chasing wealth.'

'You cared what they thought, these people you had never seen?' he asked.

'I cared what *I* thought, what *you* thought. It was better to go while I could.' April hung her head and turned away, but he turned her back, tilting her face and watching the tears that had started to fall slowly.

'I saw the plane leave,' he confessed quietly. 'I watched it climb to the clouds and leave Greece, and I was glad.' When her lips trembled he smiled for the first time, that slow secret smile that Marika had not been able to understand. 'It was then that I was sure. I knew why you had gone, why you had escaped from me and left everything behind.'

'I—I've just told you,' April whispered unhappily.

'No, you have not. You have not told me that you love me too much to be my mistress, too much to have me believe that wealth has anything to do with your feelings. You are like me. It is all or nothing. That is why I was glad to see the plane go, happy to watch you leave me.' He caught her in his arms, looking down at her, smiling into her eyes. 'I have missed you, *karithia mou*,' he whispered. 'I have missed you every minute.'

'I've missed you too. I'm unhappy away from you but I can't...'

His fingers wiped her tears as her voice choked on the words.

'I thought I was preparing the greatest surprise for you. I went inside to tell my mother that there would be two celebrations that night, two reasons for the boat to be alive with lights. I went to tell her that, like my brother, I was betrothed. When we came out to get you, you had gone, and the people in the street told me you had called a taxi. Oh, I tried to find you, it is true. I chased through the traffic with Marika urging me on but inside I knew you had left me and I knew why.'

April gazed at him spellbound, not really under-standing it all, and when he just smiled at her she touched his face timidly.

'Can you tell me in simple English?' she begged. 'Can you tell me so that an idiot could understand?'

'I want to marry you, *karithia*,' he said quietly. 'I have come to get you and take you home to Greece.'

The tears just fell faster and he pulled her close, kissing them away and then covering her lips with his own.

'I have waited for this,' he groaned, 'longed for it. Say yes, *karithia*.'

'You've said that word to me lots of times,' April reminded him shakily. 'You said it that night on the island when . . .'

'When you belonged to me,' he finished for her. 'I can say it in English. It means darling. Will you marry me, my darling? I love you too, so very much.'

'Oh, yes!' She wound her arms around his neck and he swept her off her feet, sitting with her on the settee and kissing her with a desperation that showed how much he needed her.

'We will have a celebration of our own,' he told her between urgent kisses. 'We will light the boat up with coloured lights and have enough fireworks for all Athens to see, enough guests to be dazzled by my love. Later we will send them all away and sail out to sea where nobody can find us.'

When April was flushed and breathless with his kisses, Michalis stood and lifted her into his arms.

'We will go to bed,' he said with his normal arrogance.

'It's only two in the afternoon!' April protested, but he brushed such things aside.

'I will close the curtains if you are worried. I have waited for a long time to hold you again, to own you again, and I want you now. Tonight is another matter.'

'Don't think you can boss me about,' April warned tremulously, burying her face against the strong warmth of his neck.

'I will not think it. I will not even consider it, providing that I get all my own way.' He smiled down at her. 'I do not expect there will be a battle,' he said tenderly.

April flushed softly and closed her eyes, curling against him. There had never been a battle when he kissed her.

There had only been dark magic, and she was beginning to drift into it even then.

When they were at last lying in each other's arms, Michalis looked down at her entranced face, seeing her trembling commitment, and his own eyes became glazed with passion.

'I love you,' he breathed huskily. 'And now I want that warm, dark wonder that only you can bring. I want the heat and the darkness, the brilliant stars. Is that too domineering, *karithia mou*?'

April never answered. She was already moaning his name, clinging to him, ready to leave the world with him, falling into the velvet dark as his lips crushed hers.

Later she lay contentedly in his arms as he stroked her body with loving hands.

'Have you had trouble with that wicked stepsister?' he asked softly.

'No. She's happy. Happy people don't make trouble. I feel I have a real sister now.'

'You will soon have two. Marika has been fussing every day, urging me to come for you. She behaved at the betrothal of Stella and Petros as if it were a funeral. I have never before known her to be silent.'

'It was a long time,' April said wistfully. 'Why didn't you come for me straight away?'

'The betrothal, business affairs.' He tilted her face to his. 'Time for you to come to your senses and realise you didn't love me.'

'I do love you. You know that,' April told him fiercely, and he nodded, smiling down at her.

'I know it. I knew it then but there is always this little fear.'

'You don't fear anything.'

'I fear losing you. I fear being away from you.' He suddenly grinned down at her. 'As to that, I meant to speak severely to Petros about more effort, but to my surprise Stella has already pointed out his failings, and though to her they are few he is much impressed. I think in future I will have a little more time of my own.'

'Do you think he'll stop the lies?' April asked wryly.

'I would imagine so. Stella will not allow them. She is not so sweet as all that.'

'I'm still puzzled about the houses he described on the island,' April mused. 'His great big lie had a point, but that particular lie seemed to be just silly.'

'Not entirely,' Michalis assured her with a grin. 'I wondered about that too. When I asked him he told me that he worried about you thinking he was rich. He tried to be ordinary so that you would feel safe with him. He was lonely, missing Stella, and he needed your company.'

'My motherly company? So it was a sort of inverted snobbery.' She smiled to herself. 'I'm going to have to watch your family carefully.'

'Just watch me.' He dropped a kiss on her lips, and April just went on looking up at him, quite seriously, and he looked warily at her.

'You are thinking again, darling? It is dangerous and usually leads to trouble.'

'I was wondering how I could have hated you when I first saw you,' she explained.

'I was not too pleased myself,' he confessed, leaning back and drawing her against him. 'You were not what I expected. I was waiting grimly for some glossy, grasping woman and found myself facing a clear-eyed girl. I had to believe Petros. He had seemed so sincere, so entangled with you. My mind believed it but my heart refused, and to my dismay I wanted you myself. The more

I saw of you, the more the feeling grew. You were brave, daring, and so refreshingly direct.' He smiled to himself and cuddled her close. 'You were also a constant source of amusement, and my way of life does not bring forth women like that.'

'It was infuriating how you always got the better of me,' April grumbled.

'I knew I had to. I hardly dared let you out of my sight. Are you aware that for most of the time at the house I did not sleep in case you did something so drastic that you would injure yourself? When you tried to climb down the cliff I thought I would not reach you in time.'

'Don't remind me,' April shivered, and he looked down at her sternly.

'You will take care in future,' he ordered. 'I hope this family of yours like to fly because you cannot fly here to them without me. I was extremely surprised to observe your caution today with Willis. For a moment I thought he must have got the wrong woman. My woman walks into trouble, shouts and argues. It was strange to see caution.'

'He probably thought I was mad,' April sighed. 'I wouldn't have come at all except I seem to be almost out of work. I really thought I would have to get rid of my car.'

'A very sensible decision,' he murmured drily. 'I saw it. Another source of danger. You do not need work in any case. You will go everywhere with me. It seems to me that as you rarely unpack your cases your clothes will last a long time. I can see that you are going to be very inexpensive to keep.'

April sighed and wrapped her arms around his neck, dreaming of the wonderful future with Michalis.

'I'll have to tell my mother. She's not too pleased with you. Kidnapping is not something she approves of,' she said.

'I know. I have seen her.'

April sat up and looked down at his rather self-satisfied face in total disbelief.

'But you can't have!'

'It was necessary. I had to arrange the betrothal. Just because you are English it does not mean that I will be less Greek. Your stepfather took a little time to relax,' he added, looking at her severely. 'He seemed to think I was not at all good enough for you. He was quite aggressive until I explained how much I loved you. You are getting married in Greece. They finally agreed.'

'I'm going to be pushed around,' April began with sparkling eyes, temper sitting at the back of them like a small grey fire. 'There'll be no bossy arrangements without consultation.'

'You expect me to let you have all your own way?' he enquired, pulling her down to him and capturing her gaze with dark, intense eyes. 'My life is planned and you are part of it. I want three children and the first will be a boy. Just see that you obey, Miss Stewart.' His words were breathed threateningly into her mouth and April shivered with delight, melting against him and ready to obey any orders he issued.

'You want an heir,' she said dreamily.

'I want a sign of ownership,' he corrected, his tongue tracing her lips. 'My woman, wearing my rings and carrying my child. You have already given me enough jealousy to last a lifetime. If anyone else ever looks at you…!' His ardent threat was silenced as his lips crushed hers and he turned her beneath the demanding pressure of his body.

April submitted to the passionate tyranny, but she was smiling, even though every limb trembled, and Michalis raised his head, his dark eyes searching her face.

'You have a plan?' he asked with amused suspicion.

'Only a little one,' she whispered. 'I was wondering how long it would take me to change your ways, to make you into a nice, docile husband.'

'You want one?' he asked sensuously, his narrowed, heated gaze running over her, and she shook her head helplessly. He was perfect as he was and she wouldn't want to change anything. 'I love you,' he murmured, holding her tightly. 'I want to protect you, cherish you always, adore you forever. Is that oppression?'

April never replied—she was too busy placing small, frantic kisses on his face—and Michalis never expected an answer. He crushed her in his arms and captured her eager lips with his own.

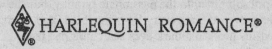

HARLEQUIN ROMANCE®

brings you

More Romances Celebrating Love, Families and Children!

Following on from Rosemary Gibson's *No Ties*,
Harlequin Romance #3344, this month we're bringing
you *A Valentine for Daisy*, Harlequin Romance #3347,
which we know you will enjoy reading! It's a wonderful
Betty Neels story, all about two adorable twins Josh and
Katie who play their part in Daisy finding true love
at last!

Watch out for these titles:

KIDSG9R

Take 4 bestselling love stories FREE

Plus get a FREE surprise gift!

Special Limited-time Offer

Mail to Harlequin Reader Service®

3010 Walden Avenue
P.O. Box 1867
Buffalo, N.Y. 14269-1867

YES! Please send me 4 free Harlequin Romance® novels and my free surprise gift. Then send me 6 brand-new novels every month, which I will receive months before they appear in bookstores. Bill me at the low price of $2.44 each plus 25¢ delivery and applicable sales tax if any*. That's the complete price and—compared to the cover prices of $2.99 each—quite a bargain! I understand that accepting the books and gift places me under no obligation ever to buy any books. I can always return a shipment and cancel at any time. Even if I never buy another book from Harlequin, the 4 free books and the surprise gift are mine to keep forever.

116 BPA ANRG

Name	(PLEASE PRINT)	
Address	Apt. No.	
City	State	Zip

This offer is limited to one order per household and not valid to present Harlequin Romance® subscribers. *Terms and prices are subject to change without notice. Sales tax applicable in N.Y.

UROM-94R   ©1990 Harlequin Enterprises Limited

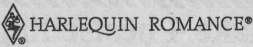

HARLEQUIN ROMANCE®

Starting in March, we are bringing you a brand-new series—**Sealed with a Kiss**. We've all written SWAK at some time on a love letter, and in these books the love story always concerns a letter—one way or another!

We've chosen RITA nominee Leigh Michaels's *Invitation to Love* (Harlequin Romance #3352) as the first title and will be bringing you one every month, right through to Christmas!

Watch for *Invitation to Love* by Leigh Michaels in March. And don't miss any of these exciting **Sealed with a Kiss** titles, by your favorite Harlequin Romance authors:

April	#3355	Dearest Love	Betty Neels
May	#3360	P.S. I Love You	Valerie Parv
June	#3366	Mail-Order Bridegroom	Day Leclaire
July	#3370	Wanted: Wife and Mother	Barbara McMahon

Available wherever Harlequin books are sold.

SWAK-G